Santa
Brought a Son

MELISSA McCLONE

Marrying
The Boss's
Daughter

SILHOUETTE *Romance*®

Published by Silhouette Books

America's Publisher of Contemporary Romance

Special thanks and acknowledgment are given to Melissa McClone for her contribution to MARRYING THE BOSS'S DAUGHTER series.

For Rose

SILHOUETTE BOOKS

ISBN 0-373-19698-9

SANTA BROUGHT A SON

Visit Silhouette at www.eHarlequin.com

Printed in U.S.A.

Books by Melissa McClone

Silhouette Romance

If the Ring Fits… #1431
The Wedding Lullaby #1485
His Band of Gold #1537
In Deep Waters #1608
The Wedding Adventure #1661
Santa Brought a Son #1698

Yours Truly

Fiancé for the Night

MELISSA McCLONE

With a degree in mechanical engineering from Stanford University, the last thing Melissa McClone ever thought she would be doing is writing romance novels, but analyzing engines for a major U.S. airline just couldn't compete with her "happily-ever-afters."

When she isn't writing, caring for her three young children or doing laundry, Melissa loves to curl up on the couch with a cup of tea, her cats and a good book. She enjoys watching home-decorating shows to get ideas for her house—a 1939 cottage that is *slowly* being renovated.

Melissa lives in Lake Oswego, Oregon, with her own real-life hero husband, two daughters, son, two lovable but oh-so-spoiled indoor cats and a no-longer-stray outdoor kitty who decided to call the garage home. Melissa loves to hear from readers. You can write to her at P.O. Box 63, Lake Oswego, OR 97034.

FROM THE DESK OF EMILY WINTERS

~~Six~~ Three Bachelor Executives To Go

Bachelor #1: Love, Your Secret Admirer
Matthew Burke—Hmm...his sweet ~~assistant~~ clearly has googly eyes for her ~~workaholic boss.~~ Maybe I can make some office ~~magic~~ happen.

Bachelor #2: Her Pregnant Agenda
Grant Lawson—The guy's ~~a dead~~ ringer for Pierce Brosnan— who ~~wouldn't~~ want to fall into his strong, protective arms?

Bachelor #3: Fill-in Fiancée
Brett Hamilton—The ~~playboy~~ from England is really a British lord! ~~Can I~~ find him a princess...or has he found her already?

Bachelor #4: Santa Brought a Son
Reed Connors—The ambitious VP seems to have a heavy heart. Only his true love could have broken it. But where is she now?

Bachelor #5: Rules of Engagement
Nate Leeman—Definitely a lone wolf kind of guy. A bit hard around the edges, but I'll bet there's a tender, aching heart inside.

Bachelor #6: One Bachelor To Go
Jack Devon—The guy is so frustratingly elusive. Arrogant and implacable, too! He's going last on my matchmaking list until I can figure out what kind of woman a mystery man like him prefers....

Prologue

As "Jingle Bells" played from speakers hidden among the fake snow and icicles at the mall's version of the North Pole, Timmy Wilson stared at the line of kids waiting to visit Santa Claus. He was almost eight years old, too old to believe in Santa, let alone sit on his lap, but Grandma told him this was important to his mom so here he was.

"Tell Santa what you want for Christmas," Grandma said.

"Shouldn't Santa know what every kid wants?"

Grandma sighed. "That's what your father used to say."

Timmy missed his dad more than anything. He'd been in Heaven for three years, and Timmy figured his dad must play baseball everyday up there. "I wish he was here and could teach me how to throw a curve ball."

She blinked. "Me, too, Timmy. Me, too."

A girl, wearing an elf's costume and pointy shoes, led him to Santa, who sat in a large chair. It sort of reminded Timmy of a king's throne. This Santa had a real beard and small gold-rimmed glasses. His fancy red suit looked new, and his black leather boots shone. Much better than the Santa from the Main Street Thanksgiving Parade.

Timmy glanced around hoping none of his little league teammates were at the mall, too. He could just imagine the teasing he'd get if they saw him.

"Would you rather sit or stand?" Santa asked.

"Stand," Timmy admitted, "but the picture is for my mom and she'd probably like me on your lap."

Santa patted his knee. "Climb up. We'll make it fast."

Timmy sat on Santa's lap. It wasn't so bad. This Santa didn't wear padding. He also smelled good, sort of like a candy cane and a cookie.

Mrs. Claus stood behind a camera. "Smile."

The flash blinded Timmy. He rubbed his eyes.

"What do you want for Christmas?" Santa asked.

"I already sent you a letter." The picture had been taken. Now all Timmy wanted was to be done so he could get a smoothie. "After Thanksgiving."

"That's right. You asked for a Gameboy Advance, a skateboard and a book on pitching." Santa's blue eyes twinkled. "But there's something else you want, something you haven't told anyone about."

No way. He couldn't know that. Not unless he had super-mind-reading power or if he was the real thing. And if he was the real Santa…Timmy felt all shivery inside like the time Grandpa let him eat chocolate cake with ice cream for breakfast. He nodded. "Can you…"

"That's a big request," Santa answered before Timmy could get the words out. "I'll try, but I might need a little help. It's a busy time of year. Maybe an elf could help me out. Or an angel." Santa adjusted his glasses. "Christmas *is* a time for miracles. Do you believe in miracles, Timmy?"

"I'll believe in anything if it gets me a new dad."

Chapter One

The wedding invitation sat in the middle of Reed Connors's desk. The embossed ivory card should have blended in with the other pieces of paper competing for his attention, but the invitation might as well have been printed on orange fluorescent paper. No way could he ignore it any longer.

Reed had received the invitation a month ago. His best friend from high school was getting married. But Reed had been too busy to reply, had shoved the damn thing in his briefcase and forgotten about it. Until now.

He replayed the voice mail message.

"Hey, Reed, it's Mark Slayter," his best friend's familiar voice said. "Long time no see, bud. I know you're busy, but we're trying to get a final head count for the caterer so I need to know whether you're coming to the wedding or not. All the guys will be there and we'd love to see you. It's been too long. Don't know if it makes a difference, but Samantha Wilson will be there, too. I know you remember her, even if you forgot the rest of us losers. Take care, dude, and let me know ASAP."

Mark would mention Samantha Brown Wilson. No one else knew about Reed's special friendship with the most beautiful, most popular girl at Fernville High School, and Mark had never told a soul, even though the group of nerds they'd hung out with pretty much shared everything. Reed had never had a friend as loyal as Mark had been. Reed doubted he ever would.

Thinking back, he remembered what a fool he'd been with Samantha—a lovesick fool. Not surprising. He'd been the stereotypical geek and could have written the book on being a high school loser. He'd come a long way since then.

As Reed stared at his schedule for December, he tapped his pen against a stack of manila folders. The rapid tattoo helped him concentrate when he brainstormed the newest marketing strategy and tried to build brand equity for Wintersoft Software, but in this case it was only making an annoying sound. A trip to Frankfurt, a conference in San Jose, a tradeshow in Las Vegas. Meetings with investment analysts. A trip to Fernville, Virginia, for Mark's wedding was impossible.

"Working late...again?" A cheery, feminine voice asked from the doorway of his office.

He didn't have to look up to know it was Carmella Lopez, Executive Assistant to CEO Lloyd Winters. She reminded him of everyone's favorite aunt except she dressed like the perfect professional in stylish jacket and skirt ensembles, cooked the most amazing rice and beans this side of the Rio Grande and was easier to confide in than an anonymous bartender.

"It's not that late." Reed glanced out the window behind him and saw lights from the other Boston skyscrapers in the night sky. He'd not only missed the sunset, but dinner. Worse, he was still wearing his jacket and tie. "Lost track of time."

"Seems to be a habit of yours." The warmth of her smile echoed in her voice.

"You shouldn't talk. You're here, too."

"Lloyd likes me to be around when he's in the office."

"You treat him too well."

"He's a good…boss."

"Exactly." Reed grinned. "Don't want the boss to think I'm a slackard."

"With the hours you put in, no one would think that." She walked to his desk and handed him a folder. "Lloyd wants you to review the latest info on the Utopia project."

Reed placed it on the top of the media plan and advertising-effectiveness reports in his jam-packed in box and made a mental note to call Nate Leeman, Senior V.P. of Technology, to see if Utopia was on schedule or not. "I'll read it tonight."

"It's already so late." Carmella's gaze clouded with concern. "You have to sleep sometime."

"Who needs sleep when I have all this?" He motioned to his office full of artwork from the countries he'd traveled to with his job—a job he loved more than anything. Ensuring Wintersoft's product names and marketing strategies were meaningful and translatable into all markets and cultures was challenging. Dealing with all the planning surrounding a new product's introduction when he could never count on the delivery date could be a huge headache and stress, but he wouldn't change a thing. At twenty-eight, he was the youngest V.P. at the company and he wasn't about to stop there.

She pointed to the top of Reed's cluttered desk. "Is that a wedding invitation?"

He nodded. Carmella stuck her nose into everyone's business, but he didn't mind. She truly cared about her co-workers and dispensed advice with motherly warmth.

"Is another V.P. getting married?"

"Not that I know of." In the past three months, three of Wintersoft's male executives had gotten married or engaged. First Matt Burke, then Grant Lawson and the latest, Brett Hamilton. The whole thing made Reed wary. Marriage was the last thing on his mind. Work left little time for casual dating, let alone anything more serious. "Brett had better be the last one or I'm going to stop drinking the water around here."

"Now that Arianna has had her twins, we'll have to see if that's in the water, too."

"Not funny." A girlfriend was a time drain, but children? Forget it. His job left no room for a family. He had the perfect life. Why spoil a good thing?

"So who's getting married?" Carmella asked.

"My best friend from high school."

"Sounds like fun."

About as much fun as a four-day marketing blitz through ten European countries with your boss at your side. "I'm not going."

Carmella sat in the chair opposite his desk. "Why not?"

"Too busy." Work was the way to achieve all he wanted. Reed had tasted success and wanted more. That took a sacrifice—his personal life—but it was worth it. "I'll send a nice gift."

"But if he was your best friend..."

Reed shrugged, though blowing off Mark's wedding might be a bigger deal than Reed was making it. "I was close to Mark and the few others we hung out with, but we all drifted apart after high school."

"He still invited you," Carmella said. "That has to count for something."

"I get invited to a lot of weddings." Reed stared at the invitation. "Co-workers, work-related acquaintances who just want something from me."

"Your friend only wants a day. That isn't a lot to ask of a best friend."

"If I didn't have so much work—"

She tsked. "Work is an excuse."

Reed didn't—couldn't—answer. Carmella had a way of seeing through a person. She considered it a gift, but on more than one occasion, like now, he wished she'd returned it and exchanged it for another.

"It's the same one you used when I asked why you haven't been in a serious relationship since you started at Wintersoft."

"I date," he said finally.

"But never the same woman."

"Nothing wrong with that."

"There is if you don't want to spend the rest of your life alone." She stared at him with an observant gleam in her eyes. "I'm wondering if there isn't another reason. The only woman you've mentioned by name is Samantha, your high school sweetheart. I know that was years ago, but are you sure you got over her?"

"Yes."

Carmella didn't look convinced.

"Samantha wasn't my sweetheart," Reed admitted. Only in his dreams had she been his. Except for six wonderful days. "We were only together a short time when I was in college. I was too much of a geek to have a girlfriend in high school. Brainy not brawny."

"You must have been a late bloomer because you have both now."

"Thanks." Reed had struggled and worked hard to become the man he was today.

"So...will she be at the wedding?"

"Yes." He thought about Samantha. Her long, silky blond hair. Her sparkling blue eyes. Her warm, seductive laughter. Reed's collar felt a little tight. He loosened his tie. "And so will her husband," he added more for his benefit than Carmella's.

Her eyes widened. "Samantha got married? When?"

"I'm not sure. She was two years younger than me." But Reed knew who she'd married—Art Wilson, the one she'd chosen over him. In a way, Reed owed Samantha. If she had chosen him instead, he doubted he would have been so focused in college and in making his dreams a reality.

"When was the last time you saw her?"

"Spring break of my sophomore year of college," he answered. "That's the last time I was in Fernville. Once my parents moved here to Boston and my friends went away to college, there was no reason to go back."

"Your friend's wedding sounds like a very good reason."

Patrick, Wes and Dan would probably attend, too. Reed hadn't seen them in years. Or Mark for that matter. The wedding would be a lot of fun. Reed stared at his schedule. There had to be a way....

Carmella picked up the response card. "You've missed the deadline, but don't let that stop you."

If Reed sent someone else to the conference in San Jose, he would free up enough time to go to the wedding. "I won't."

As she handed him the response card, her brow wrinkled. "So you're going to the wedding?"

Reed smiled. "I'm going."

"He's going," Carmella whispered to Emily Winters when she stepped into the crowded elevator about to descend from the fiftieth floor.

Emily knew the "he" in question was Reed Connors. Handsome, ambitious and a few years younger than her— Reed was not only a co-worker, but also one of the potential husband candidates her father most likely had in mind. No way did she want her father telling any of her fellow co-workers they should take an interest in her. Talk about embarrassing. Not to mention the fact she wasn't interested in getting married, period.

The other passengers exited on the forty-ninth floor. The doors closed. Emily hit the stop button. No one could eavesdrop on them here. "What about the girl from Reed's hometown?"

"She's going, too," Carmella admitted. "But she got married."

So much for that plan. Emily massaged her temples.

"Who knows if she's still married," Carmella said. "But if she is, Reed needs to get her out of his system so he can fall in love with someone else. He's not as over her as he thinks."

"And if she's not married?"

"Then your job got a whole lot easier." Carmella laughed. "Chances are we'd have one less bachelor to worry about."

Emily sighed. "If only we didn't have to worry about any of them."

"I agree, but we're halfway there." Excitement filled Carmella's voice. "Three bachelors down, three to go."

She made it sound so easy, and in a way it was. Carmella researched the men using their personnel files, and Emily found them their perfect match. But she hated having to resort to this. "I guess."

Carmella's brown eyes narrowed. "Isn't this what you wanted? To make sure all six of the single male executives were off the market so your father couldn't marry you off to one of them?"

Emily hesitated, torn by conflicting emotions. "Yes, but this whole matchmaking plan seems so crazy. I've been feeling…selfish."

"Have you considered the alternative?" Carmella asked.

"Yes. And I'm not going to marry one of the three remaining bachelors." Emily raised her chin. "They're great guys, but I'm not ready to settle down. I just got the promotion and I need to concentrate on my career."

"Work won't keep you warm on a cold winter's night."

A smile tugged on the corners of Emily's lips. "You sound like my father."

"He loves you."

"I know," she said. "That's why he's so concerned about my marital status. But I already made the mistake of letting him pick out one husband from the company roster. I don't want to spend the rest of my life alone, but I won't marry another co-worker that he chooses for me."

"Speaking of your ex-husband, Todd stopped by to see me."

"Me, too."

Carmella raised an arched brow. "And?"

"Nothing," Emily admitted. "He's upset over losing his job. The golden boy's rocket isn't climbing so high anymore and he doesn't know what to do about it."

"That's not your fault."

"If we hadn't gotten married he'd still be working here and wouldn't have had to take a job with another company and be laid off." Frustration laced each of her words. Worry creased her forehead. "I wish my father understood why I don't want to get into that situation again. It's humiliating and wrong."

"You mean the world to your father, Emily. He'd never do anything on purpose to embarrass you."

"Then he should realize I'll marry when I'm ready." She pulled the stop button out and the elevator descended. "Not anytime before that."

"What about our plan?" Carmella asked. "Should I keep researching the final three or stop?"

Doubts swirled in Emily's mind. She thought about the three remaining bachelor executives: Reed Connors, Nate Leeman and Jack Devon. Nate was a brilliant workaholic who seemed to live at the office. Jack was a ladies' man according to Boston Magazine, who named him one of the city's "Fifty Hottest Bachelors," and a mystery to all who worked with him. And Reed worked hard and had lofty ambitions that could play right into her father's hand. "Let's see what happens with Reed first."

Samantha Wilson stood midway up the aisle of the empty church holding the bridesmaid bouquet she'd found on the altar and surveyed her hard work. On the end of each pew, a miniature wreath decorated with tiny berries, cinnamon sticks and pinecones hung from red-and-green-plaid ribbon tied in bows. At the front of the church, potted red and white poinsettias created a cascading effect on the steps leading up to the altar. And the altar was decorated with fresh pine boughs and garland. Pinecones, holly, berries and the same red-and-green-plaid ribbon from the pew wreaths provided a splash of color and texture to the greenery that filled the church with a christmasy pine scent.

A satisfied feeling settled in the center of her chest. The bride and groom had wanted a Christmas wedding theme, and Samantha had done her best to give it to them. Not only here, but at the reception site, too.

She ran through her mental checklist. Almost everything was ready. Soon the church would be filled with friends and family, witnesses to Mark Slayter's and Kelli Jefferson's exchange of wedding vows.

A lump formed in Samantha's throat. As a girl, she'd dreamed about having a big wedding in a church overflowing with everyone she'd ever known, walking down the aisle with her father, wearing a white gown fit for a fairy princess. But reality had been a wedding at city hall with

only her future in-laws, Helen and Frank Wilson, in attendance. Samantha's parents hadn't given her the courtesy of
an RSVP. The only white on the floral-print dress she'd
normally worn to church had been the collar.

No diamond ring or bouquet of roses or exotic honeymoon, either. She touched Helen's strand of pearls for a
moment and let go of them. So she didn't get the wedding
of her dreams. She got something much better.

Samantha noticed a crooked bow on a pew wreath. She
shifted the bouquet to her left hand and adjusted the ribbon
until it was perfect.

"Sam?"

The name echoed in the church and she froze. No one
had called her that in years. As she glanced toward the
back, a man in a navy suit stepped from the vestibule. Dark-
brown hair, warm chocolate eyes and a smile that made her
legs feel like wilted rose stems. She tightened her grip on
the bouquet. "Y-y-yes."

"It *is* you," Reed Connors said.

The closer he came, the harder it was to breathe. She
clutched the end of a pew and took deep breaths until she
was strong enough to face him.

His looks had matured. His nose was the same, straight
except for a bump where he'd gotten hit with a snowball
junior year, but his cheekbones looked chiseled, more de-
fined. His jaw looked stronger and his lips seemed more
full. He'd grown taller and filled out, too. His suit fit perfectly, accentuating his wide shoulders and perfect posture.

"Reed." With her heart pounding in her chest, she struggled to remain calm. He'd never called, never wrote, never
returned to Fernville in almost nine years. And now to walk
back into her life… An odd combination of fear and re-
sentment made its way down her spine. "What are you
doing here?"

"Mark's wedding."

Samantha had forgotten Reed and Mark had been best friends in high school. She'd pushed that, and a million other little details from the past, to the back of her mind. Sometimes it was too painful to remember.

Reed glanced at his watch. "Look's like we're both early. Mark wanted me to stop by before the ceremony."

"I've been here for hours. I'm doing the flowers," she said a little too quickly. "I mean, I'm a guest, too, but I'm also the florist. I have my own flower shop here in town."

His eyes widened, but returned to normal in an instant. Strange, he had never been this calm and collected before. He'd been so shy and adoring whenever he helped her with homework. It had made her feel feminine and cherished. A way she hadn't felt with anyone else.

But the man standing in front of her didn't look as though he got nervous about anything or anyone. And *man* was the only way to describe him.

Reed Connors had gone from brainy looking and skinny to gorgeous and a hunk. Had it taken a kiss to turn him from frog to prince? She swallowed. Hard. Not that she had any intention of falling under his spell again.

Besides she'd never cared what he looked like. She'd seen beneath his being too thin with thick glasses and a bad case of acne to the caring person underneath. At least, she'd thought he'd cared. Thought he'd loved her. But she'd been wrong. About Reed, about so many things. She stared at the bouquet in her left hand.

"You stayed in Fernville?" he asked.

"I...I...we stayed."

She waited for him to ask about Timmy. Her son.

Their son.

But Reed didn't. Damn him. After all this time, she thought Reed would have been at least curious about Timmy. She pushed her disappointment aside for the millionth time, but a permanent sorrow bore down on her.

Reed must have ice running through his veins. Nothing else would explain his actions.

But she had to remember it was for the best. No one knew the truth about her son. No one except her, Art and Reed. And she had to keep it that way.

Reed's assessing gaze made Samantha feel tongue-tied and self-conscious in her found-on-sale-at-the-consignment-store black dress. She pushed back a stray hair that had slipped out of her French twist.

The tables had turned.

She was no longer the girl she'd been. No longer the daughter of the wealthy Browns who could never live up to the example set by her perfect older brother. Samantha had known her parents' love had to be earned, but she never thought they could harden their hearts against her so easily and kick her out of the house when she'd told them she was pregnant, a month before high school graduation. She'd been alone, penniless and homeless. Thanks to Reed, her entire life had been altered.

Shattered.

But she had picked up the pieces, and with help from Art and his parents, moved on. She was now part of the Wilson family, and had to be careful so nothing she did would change that. But Reed's presence was another living reminder of her biggest mistake. If Frank and Helen found out…Samantha squared her shoulders.

"Has life gotten more exciting here?" Reed asked.

"No, but I like it."

"You never used to like it."

"True." In high school she couldn't wait to leave the confines of Fernville. The small town had threatened to suffocate her and her dreams. Now someone would have to drag her away from the comfort of the town she fondly called home. "Things, people change."

"Not you." One corner of his mouth lifted. "You look the same. Only better."

His compliment sent an unexpected rush of emotion through her. Her cheeks warmed, and she smoothed the skirt of her dress. "You're only being polite."

"I'm not," he admitted. "You look great."

"So do you. In your suit and everything." Darn, the more she said the stupider she sounded. That wouldn't do at all. So what if he wore a designer suit and expensive leather shoes and looked like a male model? Reed, of all men, should not be having this effect on her. Not that it was really an effect. She was merely flustered by his sudden appearance. "I mean—"

"I know what you mean."

Reed and she might have been different back when, but Samantha had believed he understood her like no one else, not even Art. She could be herself and not worry whether he would like her or not. But when push came to shove, Art had been the one who'd known what she needed in a way that defied logic, not Reed. The fact he still hadn't asked about Timmy proved how little either of them had understood or known about each other. Well, she wasn't about to offer any information.

Reed glanced around. "You've done a beautiful job transforming the church into a holiday wonderland, but what happened to moving to the big city, becoming a lawyer and fighting to right the injustices of the world?"

A teenage pregnancy, being disowned by her parents, getting married the day after high school graduation, a part-time job at a grocery store and a baby at age eighteen. "Life."

"Care to elaborate?"

"Not really." He knew some of the story, but hadn't cared enough to do anything. And he still didn't care. It was better this way. She had to protect her family and would—no matter what the cost. She straightened, wishing she'd worn high heels so she could even out his height advantage. "What about you? Have you taken the business world by storm?"

"Not quite. I work for a financial software company in Boston. I'm V.P. of global marketing."

His dreams had been the most important thing in his life. More important than her and their baby. She hoped the price he'd paid was worth it. "Still planning to make your first million before you turn thirty?"

"We'll see."

No, *he* would see. There was no room for him in her life. What they had shared the spring of her senior year of high school had been like a dream—a dream come true for a few short days. He'd come back from college and she'd seen something different in him, felt things she'd never felt before and done things without a thought to the consequences or the future. Reed had swept her off her feet and stolen her heart.

Until their time together, she had never felt loved. Not by her parents who wanted her to be perfect, not by her then ex-boyfriend Art who didn't want her unless she had sex with him, not by anyone. But Reed had made her feel the way she'd longed to feel—loved only for who she was. As if no matter what she did or said, he would still love her. Or so she thought. Samantha had been wrong. Their story hadn't had a fairy-tale ending. No happily ever after for them.

But she was older and wiser. She would not repeat the mistakes of the past. And that's where Reed belonged.

In her past.

The only thing he could do in the present was destroy her life by letting the truth about Timmy come out. If he wanted to pretend he didn't have a son, fine. She was more than happy to oblige.

With her resolve firmly in place, she forced a smile. "It's been nice seeing you, but I need to return the missing bouquet to an upset bridesmaid and light the luminaries outside the church before the guests arrive."

"I'll see you later," he said.

Not if I can help it. She was going to stay as far away from Reed Connors as possible. Too much was at stake to let him near her again. "We'll see."

Reed watched Samantha walk down the aisle and into the vestibule. She looked sexy in her little black dress. The sway of her hips hypnotized him as if he were under a spell or dreaming. The slamming of a church door told him he was doing neither. He was wide awake.

He had believed he was over Samantha Brown and had gotten her out of his system years ago. He had.

Samantha Wilson, however, was another story. Such a beauty. Her bright, blue eyes contained an intriguing soulfulness. He was itching to pull the pins from her blond hair to see whether she'd cut the length to match her new matter-of-fact personality. Her figure had improved over the years—no cheerleader outfit necessary to show off her curves in all the right places. And she seemed more confident, self-possessed, mature. Qualities he'd never associated with her before. Qualities he found surprisingly attractive.

His system was going haywire. Talk about circuit overload. But there was no customer-service number to call. The engineering department would be no help, either. He was on his own. And for once he didn't like it.

Instead of feeling like a man in control of his own destiny, he felt like an insecure, uncertain teenager. He hated that.

He was successful, in demand, everything he wanted to

be, yet Samantha still made him feel like the dork he'd once been.

Reed took a deep breath and exhaled slowly. He couldn't allow her to get to him like this.

Once upon a time, she'd been the princess and he the court jester, strictly there for her entertainment and to make sure she didn't fail any of her classes.

But things had changed.

She was a florist in a no-nothing town, perfectly attainable if not for her marital status. He, on the other hand, was achieving all he'd dreamed about.

Reed had everything he'd ever wanted.

Everything except Samantha.

Chapter Two

As the new Mr. and Mrs. Mark Slayter finished their stroll down the aisle to the tune of Beethoven's "Ode to Joy," the bells in the steeple chimed. Reed followed the stream of wedding guests outside to the steps of the 275-year-old church. People milled about as if it were a spring afternoon, not early December with a wintry chill in the air.

"I'm Rebecca," an attractive woman with hazel-green eyes said to him. "Are you a friend of the groom or the bride?"

"The groom," Reed answered. "Rebecca Donnelly, right?"

"You know my name, but I'm positive we've never met before." She smiled seductively. "I would never forget a man like you."

"You sat next to me in physics and world history senior year." Her blank look didn't surprise him. "Reed Connors."

Her mouth gaped. "I'm sorry, Reed. I didn't recognize you."

"That's okay," he said. "I only lived in Fernville a couple of years. No reason for you to remember me."

She pursed her glossed lips. "Can I make it up to you?"

"Possibly." His hint of suggestiveness left Rebecca nodding and batting her heavily mascara-covered eyelashes.

As he made the one-block stroll to the reception, Reed searched for his friends from high school. They had to be here, but he didn't see them. He reached the reception site, the town's recreation center. An odd choice for a wedding reception considering he used to compete in chess tournaments there. The only difference between then and now was a new sign out front.

Inside, a framed picture of Mark and Kelli sat on an easel. A white mat with guests' signatures and greetings surrounded the photo. Reed picked up the pen, scribbled the words "May the force be with you as you live long and prosper together" and signed his name. Mark would understand as only a former Star Wars/Trekkie geek would.

With his seat-assignment card in hand, Reed stepped through the pine-garland-trimmed entrance to the multipurpose room and was transported from the recreation center's nondescript decor into a romantic winter wonderland.

The scent of pine permeated the air. White gauzy fabric with sparkling snowflakes on it covered the walls. Garland entwined with white lights was draped over them. Next to the dance floor stood a twelve-foot Christmas tree decorated with white lights, red bows and crystal hearts. A smiling angel, with wings spread wide, graced the top of the tall tree. Reed's assistant had sent a gift for him, and he wondered if it was under the tree with the other wedding presents.

Had Samantha done all this? The girl he remembered hadn't seemed interested in flowers unless they were for a prom corsage. Though she'd been more concerned about whether they clashed with the color and style of her dress.

But Reed had thought he'd seen more in her. Too bad he'd been wrong.

Reed passed a group of carolers dressed like characters from a Dickens novel and made his way to the other side of the room. He located table four.

"Hey." Reed was happy to see three of his closest friends from high school and two women seated here. "I've been wondering where you guys were. It's been a long time."

"I don't believe it." Wes Harkens, who had a goatee and a lot less hair than Reed remembered, rose from his seat and shook his hand. "Mark said you were coming, but I didn't see you at the church so I thought you hadn't made it."

"I was with Mark until right before the ceremony," Reed said, thinking how good it had been to catch up on the past eight years with his old friend. "Mark was as cool as a cucumber, but once I saw Kelli, I understood."

As his three buddies nodded knowingly, the attractive brunette sighed. "Don't you guys think about anything else?"

"Sorry, honey. We don't." Dan Crenshaw, as tall as ever, but no longer as skinny as a twig, laughed. "I thought a million-dollar deal would spring up and keep you away, Reed."

He smiled. "I don't make the deals, just make sure everyone knows about them and Wintersoft."

"But you must be doing well. Wintersoft is a great company." Patrick Fitzgerald, who looked eighteen not twenty-eight, hugged him. "Good to see you, Reed."

"You, too," he said.

The introductions continued. Reed met Dan's fiancée, Jenn, and Wes's wife, a pregnant, auburn-haired beauty named Claire. For two guys who'd never dated in high school, they had done well in the spouse department. Pat-

rick, who hadn't outgrown his thick black-rimmed glasse
and too-short pants, seemed to have come alone, but tw
empty seats at the table still remained.

"Looks like we'll have all the single women to our
selves," Reed said to Patrick.

"Maybe you will."

"Thank goodness," a familiar feminine voice said. "
never thought I'd find it."

One glance and Reed's heart skipped a beat. He felt th
same way he had the first time Samantha had bounced int
the computer lab in her short cheerleader skirt and tigh
sweater asking for help with her algebra homework. Sh
had never meant to be a tease, but she had been a natura
flirt who drove all males, regardless of age, to the brink o
insanity.

"Table four." She glanced at her table-assignment car
and at each of the table's occupants. Her gaze lingered o
Reed for a moment longer than the others, and he wondere
if anyone else noticed or saw the wariness in her eyes
"Looks like I'm at the right place."

All three of his friends stared at Samantha with the sam
look of awe they had in high school. Patrick nearly tripped
over himself to pull out her chair. He pushed his glasse
up the bridge of his nose. "Here you go, Samantha."

Her face glowed with a radiance Reed didn't remember
Must be the lighting. No one could look that good.

"Thank you," she said.

Patrick's red cheeks brought back so many memorie
about Samantha for Reed. His senior year he'd hacked int
the school computer system to get her class schedule. Th
first day back at school he'd managed to "bump" into he
between every class, but more than once he'd been too sh
to say anything but hello. He'd been so pathetic. At leas
that was in the past.

Reed sat, leaving an empty seat between him and Sa

antha. The smart thing to do, he told himself, even though
he idea of sitting next to Art Wilson— the man who had
ormented him through high school and married the girl of
eed's teenaged dreams—didn't thrill him, but he was an
dult and no longer in a losing competition. He could han-
le it. And Art.

Samantha picked up her flute of champagne. "Wasn't
he ceremony lovely?"

"I cried," Claire admitted.

"You cry during commercials. Even when you aren't
regnant." Jenn laughed. "The bridesmaid dresses are gor-
eous."

"They are beautiful, but now you can see why I told
Kelli no when she asked me to be a bridesmaid?" Claire
atted her big-enough-to-burst belly. "I'm much too big to
rance around in a sexy bridesmaid dress."

"You're all baby." Wes's voice, so soft and full of af-
ection, was a 180 degrees different from when he used to
alk like Commander Data from *Star Trek: The Next Gen-
ration.* "You look beautiful."

Claire shrugged. "Thanks, but I didn't want an album of
edding party pictures showing how 'beautiful' and big I
ook."

"These are nice." Dan adjusted the centerpiece, a small
ine wreath circling a vanilla-scented candle. "I can't wait
o see what you do for our wedding, Samantha."

"She won't be able to top what she did at ours," Wes
dmitted while Claire agreed.

Samantha's eyes reflected her gratitude. "Thanks, but I
nly did what Kelli and Mark wanted done."

Reed watched the exchange in amazement. The entire
able acted as if they were friends, not acquaintances. He
idn't get it. Samantha would have never been caught dead
alking to any of these guys in high school. She had been
ice to him and treated him differently from others who

weren't in her clique. She'd made him feel special, but he'
helped her pass all her freshman and sophomore math an
science courses. He'd believed friendship had grown fro
the tutoring. They'd been an odd pair—the beauty an
brain—sharing their dreams for the future and what the
wanted out of life. They had exchanged letters once he le
for college until spring break of his sophomore year whe
they'd become lovers and the truth about how she felt—
rather didn't feel—about him came out.

The DJ announced the arrival of the bride and groom
Mr. and Mrs. Mark Slayter, and the wedding gues
clapped. A harpist took over from the carolers, and a si
down prime rib dinner was served. The conversation neve
lagged. Reed's friends wanted to know about his job an
life in Boston. After that, stories about their high scho
days and being pathetic geeks kept them entertained. S
mantha didn't talk much.

He stared at her. She was so elegant, so stunning. H
gaze drifted to her lips. He remembered every contou
every detail of those soft lips, even her taste. He remem
bered so much more about her, about the days and the nig
they had spent together. Too bad it hadn't meant the sam
to her as it had to him. Reed reached for his glass of ic
water.

What he needed was a strong dose of reality. Somethin
to remind him Samantha was no longer on the market an
put an end to the fantasy forming in his mind.

"Where's Art?" Reed asked her. "At home with th
kids?"

Everyone at the table stared at Samantha. Not even th
crystal-handled cake knife could cut through the tension.

Wes started to speak, but Samantha interrupted hin
"I—it's okay. I'll do it."

"Do what?" Reed asked, feeling like the last one t
learn a worm virus was about to destroy his hard drive.

She toyed with the edge of her napkin. "Art was involved in a motorcycle accident three years ago, and his injuries were too severe. He died."

Reed felt as if he'd been punched in the solar plexus. He also felt like a jerk. "I'm sorry. I had no idea."

"You had no reason to know."

But he should have known. Reed glanced at her bare ring finger. How could he not have noticed before? Why hadn't he asked about Art earlier? But then again, Reed had believed Samantha was living a happily ever after like she'd dreamed about. "You doing okay?"

The question sounded ridiculous once the words were out, but he'd felt compelled to say something.

Her steady gaze met his. "I'm doing fine."

Fine.

Samantha deserved better than that. But it wasn't up to him to give it to her. He knew that, both logically and realistically. Art might be out of the picture, but so was Reed. His flight was leaving tomorrow. His life was in Boston.

But you're here now.

So what? He'd come to Fernville to have fun. He wasn't looking for a second chance. Maybe a fling...

Samantha rose. "The lights on the tree are flickering. I need to fix them."

"Want some help?" Patrick asked.

"Thanks, but it's happened before and I know what to do."

As Samantha walked away, Claire sighed. "Come on, you guys. Don't make her do it alone."

"Reed?" Jenn suggested.

"Be right back." Reed stood. He should have done this on his own. Proactive, not reactive. That's how he handled things now, but around Samantha he felt a little unsure and

awkward, reminding him of his high school days. It didn'
make sense.

Standing at the tree, she tightened the miniature bulbs.

"Can I help?" he asked.

"No, thanks." She didn't glance up. "I've got it unde
control."

Reed wished he could say the same. He touched one o
the crystal hearts on the tree. Time to pull himself together
Samantha shouldn't have him reverting to his former in
securities. Okay, she was beautiful, but he'd dated beautifu
women before. Must be guilt over bringing up Art. I
couldn't be anything else. "I wanted to apologize for wha
I said back at the table."

"No need."

"I'm still sorry." He checked for a loose bulb on the
string of lights. "I would never want to cause you any
pain."

"Now that's a good one."

Her bitterness surprised him. She's the one who didn'
want him. Perhaps she was having regrets. "I know it wa
a long time ago, but we once meant something to each
other."

"Did we?"

"Yes, we did." At least he had thought so.

She raised a shoulder. "All that was a big mistake."

Just as he'd assumed, their time together had meant noth
ing to her. "A mistake," he repeated.

"I knew you would agree."

But he didn't. Not really. Being with Samantha had bee
both the best and the worst time of his life. A time o
wonder and love. A time of rejection and disappointment
But he wouldn't call it a mistake. Perhaps a lesson learned
"Sam—"

"Found it." She fiddled with the wires, and the light
stayed on. "No more flickering."

Reed wished he could say the same thing about his feelings for Samantha. His emotions seemed to be flickering on and off, and he didn't know how to fix that.

"The bride and groom want to be on their way, so let's get all the single women on the dance floor for the bouquet toss," the DJ announced.

"That's my cue to get the bride her bouquet. Excuse me." Samantha rose, grateful for a valid reason to get away from Reed if only for a few minutes. She'd been upset at his returning to Fernville, but now she was annoyed at him. She hated the pity in his eyes. His need to apologize for bringing up Art.

So she was a widow? It wasn't by choice, but she'd learned to live with it. Because of Timmy, she'd had no choice.

Timmy. The thought of her son filled her with warmth. Like her own parents, Reed had made the wrong choice where his child was concerned. He hadn't wanted to be any part of Timmy's life. Or hers. She wondered if he ever had regrets. She wondered if her own parents did. Not that it mattered. She'd only been wanted and loved on their terms. She and Timmy were better off without them in their lives.

She picked up the smaller throw-away bouquet made with fire-and-ice roses and sprigs of pine and made her way through the crowded room to the dance floor. The sweet scent of the roses tickled her nostrils, reminding her this was a wedding not a wake. She was here to enjoy herself. No sense letting Reed Connors get to her. He wouldn't be in Fernville forever. He didn't care enough to cause problems. Time to stop overreacting. Didn't she deserve a night out and some fun?

At the dance floor, Samantha handed the bouquet to a beaming Kelli. "Here you go."

"Thanks." Kelli sniffed the roses. "Make sure you stand where I can see you."

"Okay." But it was far from okay. Getting stung by a bee would be less painful than battling the other women for a chance at the bouquet, but Samantha wasn't about to disappoint her friend. She stood on the parquet dance floor, trying not to get jostled by a woman dressed in a hot pink dress, who jockeyed for a better position.

"One, two…" Before the DJ reached three, Kelli tossed the bouquet over her right shoulder. The flowers soared through the air. A woman in a teal suit reached up, but was a second too late. The bouquet landed right in Samantha's hands. She stared at the white roses with the red tips. Their coy scent wasn't so sweet now, but Kelli was clapping and smiling. That's the only thing that mattered.

Samantha clutched the bouquet to her chest and grinned at her friend. "I can't believe my luck," she said dryly.

As she walked off the dance floor, Mark removed the garter from Kelli's left leg while men whistled and cheered. The DJ counted down again. On three, Mark fired the blue satin garter over his shoulder and into the crowd of bachelors. As the garter approached, the men backed away. The garter arced toward the floor when a hand snagged it out of the air.

"Whoever caught that wanted it bad," Claire said.

She was such a romantic. Samantha knew better. "He probably had too much to drink and doesn't realize what he's done."

As Reed approached, he twirled the garter on his finger.

Jenn raised a finely arched brow. "You caught the garter?"

"I promised Mark if no one tried to catch it, I would." Reed placed the garter on his arm. "Wedding traditions mean a lot to Kelli, and Mark didn't want her to be disappointed."

Tears glistened in Claire's eyes. "That is so sweet."

Samantha couldn't believe it. Reed sounded so much like

the boy she'd known in high school she felt a tug on her heart.

"Would the pair who caught the garter and bouquet please join the bride and groom on the dance floor?" the DJ asked.

No, she couldn't. A momentary panic sent her rising from her chair. Reed stood also. Mark waved at them; Kelli grinned. At least the bride and groom were happy about this.

It wasn't a big deal, Samantha told herself as Reed led her back to the dance floor. One dance at a wedding in front of more than 150 people meant nothing. She repeated that to herself when he placed one hand on her shoulder and held her hand with the other. And repeated it again as they swayed to the music—a romantic ballad from one of the summer's biggest movies.

It was only a dance.

Too bad it didn't feel that way.

Reed's arms weren't around her pulling her close, but they might as well have been. His warmth and strength seeped into her. Shivery sensations shot through her. Dancing with him felt like second nature. A nature better left untapped, a little voice cautioned. But she ignored it. Samantha had been alone for so long, she'd forgotten how nice it felt to dance and be held. His gentle touch sent tingles up her arm and down to the tips of her black leather pumps. Nerve endings came alive. Her heart, too. It went against all reason, but she hoped this once the song was a long one.

Glancing up at Reed, her breath caught in her throat. Years ago, she'd dreamed of being on the dance floor with him at a wedding. Their wedding. But like all dreams, hers hadn't come true. And she had one person to blame. She looked away.

"Ladies and gentlemen," the DJ announced. "Let's give

the couple dancing under the mistletoe some encouragement?''

Guests tapped flatware against their glasses. Because of the clinking, Samantha assumed the DJ meant the bride and groom, but Kelli smiled and pointed toward the ceiling. Samantha didn't have to look up to know what was above her and Reed. She'd been the one to hang the mistletoe on the dance floor.

Reed's eyes darkened. "Shall we?"

No. That's the last thing she wanted to do. Now or ever.

But one brief kiss was nothing more than a holiday tradition. And it would mean a lot to Kelli. One peck wasn't about to set the town gossips' tongues wagging. Or change anything. Past, present, future. "Why not?"

She waited for Reed to take the lead. He lowered his mouth to hers. The moment his lips touched her, sensation rocketed through her. Electric shock, chemical reaction, you name it—she felt it. Talk about a swoonworthy kiss. If Reed hadn't wrapped his arm around her she would have fallen. She waited for him to back away but he didn't.

Stop, she should stop.

But kissing him felt so good. So right. So perfect.

He wasn't stopping. She didn't want to stop, either. His taste intoxicated her, a dangerous elixir that should be marked off-limits. His scent hadn't changed over the years and reminded her of the magical kisses they'd shared before.

Memories rushed back. Buried emotions, too. The years faded. The distance between them seemed to disappear.

More, she wanted more.

She leaned into him. Reed took the hint and pulled her closer. Her breasts pressed against his firm chest. Strong, he was stronger than she remembered. This wasn't a boy holding her but a man. She wished he never had to let go.

For the first time in a long while, she belonged. She could be Sam. Not Samantha. Not Mom…

Timmy.

What was she doing?

She jerked away. Applause filled the room. Samantha didn't want to guess what shade of red her cheeks were at the moment. Most likely the same color as the holly-red tablecloths or roses in Kelli's bridal bouquet. Thank goodness the lights had been turned down.

The applause continued. Reed bowed. Not to be outdone, she curtsied. If he was unaffected by the kiss and the attention, so was she. No matter she had trouble catching her breath and her hands trembled. Never mind it was all she could do not to run to the nearest exit.

"Sorry," Samantha mumbled as she made her way back to their table. "Too much champagne."

"No apology necessary, though I think the champagne had little to do with it."

She froze. "What do you mean by that?"

"It's called chemistry," he whispered, and a shiver of delight inched down her spine.

"No." She stepped away from him. "We simply got carried away."

"It wouldn't be the first time."

His words sent heat coiling within her. No, she couldn't let this happen. Not here. Not with Reed. Not again.

She tilted her chin. "But it's going to be the last."

Chapter Three

After a restless night, Reed buttoned his coat and stepped out of Marabelle Bailey's Fernville B&B. The mouthwatering aroma of freshly baked apple-cinnamon coffee cake disappeared when he shut the front door.

A light dusting of snow covered the sidewalks and tree branches. The chilly air reminded him of going to school on winter mornings like this—his boots crunching through the layers of snow and ice as he dodged snowballs thrown his way. Nerds, geeks and dweebs had made the perfect targets back then. Reed shoved his gloved hands into his jacket pockets.

A giant Christmas tree decorated with twinkling lights and large multicolored balls graced the town square. The Douglas fir towered over the garland-draped gazebo where musicians performed during the summertime. The scene was pure Currier & Ives, but Reed felt too much like Scrooge to enjoy it.

The ghosts of his past had been out in full force ever since the wedding last night. Catching up and spending time with his high school buddies had been good. He'd forgotten how much fun his friends were. But seeing Samantha after all these years and kissing her...

Something physical still existed between them. Something good. Kissing her had been better than he remembered. Better than any kiss he remembered. And this time he couldn't chalk the feeling up to inexperience. Despite his fear as a teenager that no woman would ever want him, he'd had enough practice over the years.

If Samantha had shown him any interest last night, he would have been all over it. All over her. But she wanted nothing to do with him. He'd seen it in her eyes and heard it in her voice. Her rejection was more bittersweet than painful. A relief rather than a regret. And he wasn't about to slink away without a word the way he'd done almost nine years ago. He was through being a loser. This time he would accept defeat and face her like a man. He would say goodbye, get the closure he should have gotten before and move on.

The insides of the shops surrounding the town square were dark except for the Fernville Coffee Shop and Fernville Flowers. A Closed sign hung in the window of the flower shop. Samantha stood on a ladder hanging something from the ceiling. She wore a pair of faded jeans and a gray sweater. Pink used to be her color of choice. No matter. Tastes changed over the years. What color she preferred to wear wasn't his business. Saying goodbye was. He had two hours until he needed to leave for the airport. Better get to it. Reed knocked on the glass door.

Samantha's gaze met his. No smile, no reaction at all. She climbed down from the ladder and walked to the door. Her hair was pulled back, but the style was more romantic than severe with stray tendrils framing her face. Too bad those did nothing to soften the rest of her. With the automatic movements of a robot, she unlocked the door and cracked it open. "A little early to be out and about don't you think?"

The tightness of her mouth told him she didn't want him here. He would make this quick. "I didn't get a chance to say goodbye last night."

"That hasn't stopped you before."

Her words stung, but she was right. He had ended it badly before. Hell, he hadn't even ended it. Just run away. "That's why I'm here. I wanted to say goodbye this time."

Only the cracked door separated her from him, but the silence seemed to increase the distance between them. He could hear the footsteps of someone behind him, the sound of a car's engine idling nearby and the beating of his own heart.

"That's all you want?" she asked.

He nodded.

She glanced back into the shop. Her hair was woven into a single braid. He remembered when she wore two braids. The style had been more sexy than childlike. He felt a twinge in his groin.

Don't think about her. Don't think about the past. Don't think about anything except the reason you are here.

"Okay, goodbye." She stared past him as if he were invisible. Funny, but that's how he'd felt in high school around everyone but her. "Have a safe trip back to Boston. And have a wonderful life, too."

The temperature had dropped more than a few degrees, and he couldn't blame it all on the weather. She might as well have slammed the door in his face.

"Feel better?" Samantha asked.

Reed felt the same way he had the last time he saw her. All tied up in knots and wondering what the future held without her in his life. But this time Art wasn't standing in his way. No one was. And if Reed truly wanted her, he was man enough to get her this time around. "No."

She fiddled with the door lock. "What more do you want?"

He wanted to leave. He had to return to Boston, to his job. He had no time for a long-distance relationship, let alone an affair. But something held him in his place.

Why wasn't closure enough, now that he had it? Because "goodbye" didn't resolve what they had shared so long ago. She had been his first love, his first lover. And last night's kiss had awakened both dormant feelings and memories. Good ones and bad. He realized this wasn't about saying goodbye. Not at all.

Plump snowflakes fell from the sky, landing on the sidewalk and on him. "Sam…"

"It's Samantha."

"Samantha," he repeated. "What happened during spring break—"

"Was years ago," she interrupted. "Forget about it."

Logically he knew she was correct, but Reed wanted her to admit she'd made a mistake choosing Art over him. And Reed didn't want to leave until he got that. But the longer he stood there, the better he understood it wasn't going to happen.

Snow fell harder. The darkening sky told him this wasn't a passing flurry, though the weather forecast hadn't called for snow. "Would you mind if I came inside and called the airline about my flight?"

She looked into the shop again. "This isn't a good time."

"It'll only take a minute."

With a hint of annoyance in her eyes, she stepped back and opened the door. "Okay."

It wasn't the warmest invitation he'd ever received, but he brushed the snow off him and stepped inside. "Thanks."

Her store overflowed with holiday cheer. A contrast to the reception he'd received from its owner. The scent of vanilla, cinnamon and pine reminded him of his grand-mother's house. White twinkling lights entwined in garland added a touch of whimsy. Stockings of different shapes and sizes were hung on the walls. Ornaments decorated several Christmas trees. Icicles and snowflakes dangled from the ceiling. Menorahs and dradels filled an entire display rack. Only Christmas carols were missing.

A red Santa hat lay on a table, and Reed placed it on his head. "Ho-ho-ho." He expected a smile. He didn't get one. "Nice shop. Very christmasy."

"The phone is on the counter by the cash register."

"I have my cell phone," Reed admitted. He called the airline. His flight was delayed. If the snow continued to fall, it would be canceled. Renting a car and trying to get ahead of the storm seemed like his best option. He didn't want to intrude on Samantha any longer. She'd made her choice; he was making his. He had a life now. He wasn't the same boy he'd once been.

A scream tore through the silence. A blur of blue raced from the back into the store toppling a three-foot-tall Father Christmas figurine. Samantha's quick reflexes kept it from hitting the floor.

A boy wearing a blue sweatshirt and jeans held up a Gameboy. Brown hair stuck out from his baseball cap. "Look. I made it to level six, Mom."

Mom? It shouldn't matter that she'd had a child with another man—her husband—but still Reed's heart tightened. He'd thought of her having kids, but in a detached first-comes-marriage-then-comes-baby sort of way, but seeing it was different. And affected him more than he could have imagined.

He did a double take. The kid looked too old to be hers. Guess she and Art hadn't waited to start a family.

She smiled, though her face had lost some of its color. "That's great, honey."

The tenderness in her voice took Reed by surprise. She sounded like a mom. When he was younger, he'd imagined her as a girlfriend, lover, wife, but never a mother. Of course, he'd been twenty the last time he saw her, and children hadn't been on the edge of his radar screen. The same way they weren't now.

"I didn't have to use the clues from the magazine." The boy bounced from foot to foot. "I did it all on my own."

"You'll have to teach me," she said.

Samantha eyed Reed. Her piercing gaze seemed to be searching for something. What, he didn't know.

"Okay." The boy grinned and a dimple appeared on his left cheek.

Reed touched the spot of his own dimple. Same left side.

The boy looked up at him and his smile widened. "I like your hat."

Reed had forgotten he was wearing it. "Thanks."

"My dad used to wear a Santa hat every Christmas," he said.

"Timmy, this is Mr. Connors." Samantha sounded hoarse, and she cleared her throat. "Reed, this is Timmy."

"Do you play video games?" Timmy asked.

"Yes." Reed and his high school friends had spent their free time playing video and computers games, collecting *Star Wars* figurines and watching *Star Trek* reruns and its various sequel series. "But I play more computer games now."

"Mr. Connors went to high school with me and your dad," she emphasized the last word. All of her features seemed tight. The wariness Reed had glimpsed last night was back.

"I want to be a pitcher like my dad." As Timmy drew his brows together, two lines formed about his nose. Just like Samantha used to do when she was concerned about an upcoming test or homework assignment. "But I need to learn to throw a curve ball first. Do you know how?"

"Playing catch is more my style," Reed admitted. "I never could throw a curve ball myself."

"That's okay," Timmy said. "Playing catch is fun, too. I want a new mitt for my birthday."

"When's your birthday?" Reed asked.

"In twelve days. I'll be eight." Timmy smiled. "I'm having my birthday party at the ice rink after school. We're going to skate, play hockey and eat lots of cake."

"Sounds fun."

But eight? Samantha must have gotten pregnant right after graduation. Reed subtracted nine months from Timmy's birthday. The date fell right around spring break. The spring break when they'd made love. Reed glanced at Timmy, at his brown hair and eyes. Art and Samantha had been Fernville High's blond-haired, blue-eyed golden couple. Reed's pulse quickened.

Theoretically he *could* be Timmy's father, but that wasn't possible. They'd used protection. Besides, she would have told him if he were going to be a father. No woman in her right mind would keep a child a secret. No, Timmy wasn't his. She must have gone straight from his bed to Art's, as Reed had always suspected. The truth disappointed more than hurt.

"Want to come to my party?" Timmy asked.

Samantha almost dropped a glass Santa ornament she was hanging on a tree. "That's polite of you to invite Mr. Connors, but he lives in Boston."

"Are you a Red Sox fan?" Timmy asked.

"Yes, I am."

Timmy grinned, dimple and all. "So am I."

"Mr. Connors was just leaving for the airport to catch his flight home." Her voice contained a faint tremor, and she lowered her gaze. "We shouldn't keep him any longer."

"My flight's been delayed."

She straightened. "You didn't tell me that."

"You didn't ask."

Timmy studied the screen on his Gameboy. His lips were parted and his tongue was flipped over with the tip showing between his teeth. Reed's heart slammed against his chest. That was the exact thing he did when he concentrated. One of the guys at work had pointed it out to him during a late-night poker game. Jack Devon had called it a "tell" as he watched from the sidelines while everyone else played.

It was more than a telling gesture. Timmy looked just like…

Me.

A million thoughts ran through Reed's head, but he kept coming back to one. He might have idealized her in the past, but the Samantha he'd known and loved would never keep the existence of a child—his child—from him. There had to be another explanation.

"It was nice of you to stop by, Reed." Her tone was more resigned than courteous. She moved out of the aisle to clear the way to the door. "But I'm sure you have other places you need to visit before you leave for the airport."

Reed tried to see the resemblance between him and Timmy. Tried and failed. A dimple and brown hair and eyes. Three physical traits. Not solid enough proof. Maybe Reed's mind was playing tricks on him. But that shared gesture…"Not really."

"You could come over to our house," Timmy said. "We're going to decorate our Christmas tree today. It's going to be a lot of fun. And my mom bakes cookies."

As Samantha wet her lips, her jaw tensed. "Don't forget, Mr. Connors's flight has only been delayed, not canceled."

"With this snow, it'll be canceled." Fernville was the

last place Reed expected to be for another day, but too many questions remained for him to grab his bag and hop on an airplane. "I'd love to help decorate your Christmas tree. I haven't done that in years."

She touched Timmy's shoulders and pulled him closer to her. "If the snow stops—"

"I'll catch a later flight." Reed sounded carefree, but that was the last thing he felt inside. He'd learned to control his emotions. Business required it, but it made life easier, too. One more thing he had to thank Samantha Brown Wilson for. What else, Reed wondered, was he going to learn from her while he was here?

Decorating the family Christmas tree was one of Samantha's favorite holiday traditions. Each year she brewed cider, baked batches of cookies and played carols on her compact disc player. Every year she unwrapped the ornaments, recalling the memories each held. Some happy, a few sad, others bittersweet. Not even Art's death had made her stop any of the traditions. She kept them going for Timmy's sake. And hers, too.

But today she wanted to throw everything at the tree and be done with it. That was the only way she could think to get rid of Reed Connors. Samantha sank back into the slip-covered chair she'd found at a flea market last summer and stared at the boxes of Christmas decorations and her village collection covering her living room floor.

Why was Reed here after all this time? He could ruin everything and strip the life she had worked so hard to build for her and Timmy right from under her. She loved watching a fire burn, but not when the flames were about to engulf her world. Thank goodness Helen and Frank were spending a few days in Roanoke.

As Samantha pulled another ornament from the storage box, her hand trembled. The same way her heart had been trembling since Reed stepped foot in her shop. And to think last night she'd dreamed about his kiss. She needed her head examined.

Didn't she remember what he'd done? Or rather what he hadn't done? Not once, but twice?

She took full responsibility for the first time Reed had abandoned her. She'd wanted Reed to fight for her, to prove he loved her and that she hadn't made a mistake by sleeping with him. So she'd told him Art wanted her back. Both a lie and a childish thing to do. But she'd only been eighteen at the time and feeling like giving her virginity to him had been the biggest mistake ever. She'd doubted Reed's affection. No one had loved her without strings before, why would he?

And she'd been right. Reed had been using her. He didn't fight for her, didn't ask her to stay with him, didn't do anything except skip town without a word to her.

But the second time he abandoned her and her baby was all his doing. She'd gotten over his walking out on her, but she would never understand how he could walk out on their baby. Reed had never contacted her about Timmy. It was as if his son had never existed. Until today.

She noticed Reed staring at Timmy. Was he regretting his actions now that he'd met his son? She held on to the ornament with two hands.

"What do you think, Mom?" Timmy asked.

Samantha couldn't ruin today for her son. It wasn't his fault he'd invited Reed. Timmy was being polite and didn't know better. If only she hadn't taught her son manners....

She stared at the noble fir tree and forced a smile. "It's looking great. And not one broken ornament."

"We're not done yet," Reed said.

His words surprised Samantha. He'd been so quiet since arriving at her house.

Timmy giggled, but not even the peel of his laughter

could cut through the tension. Tension no one else seemed to notice.

She unwrapped tissue from the ornament in her hands, a pair of doves on top of a sterling silver heart with the words Our First Christmas and the year they were married engraved on it. It had been a Christmas present from Art. As always, he'd put great thought and care into selecting her the perfect gift. She'd gotten him something practical—a tool belt to wear for his cabinetmaking apprenticeship.

Samantha wanted to cry for all of them, including Reed. Instead she held the ornament out to him. "Why don't you put this on the tree?"

As he studied the ornament, a muscle ticked on his neck. His expression grew taut. Reed had no reason to be upset. He was the one who walked out on them. She'd been alone, without a place to live and no means to support herself. Art had not only given her a way out; he'd given her his love.

She glanced at the Santa snow globe sitting on the center of the fireplace mantel with Christmas village pieces on either side of it. A whimsical, silly item, with a jolly Santa and a windmill, that played "Winter Wonderland." The windmill lit up and spun, sending snow piling up on Santa until he was covered from head to toe. Timmy loved it. So did Samantha.

It was the first decoration they put out every year. The snow globe was a symbol of everything Art had done for them. He had purchased it the day before Timmy's birth. Art had apologized to her, though he'd done nothing wrong. He wanted to make up for Reed not wanting her and the baby. It wasn't the first time Art had done that, nor had it been the last.

"I see a bare spot above the snowman." Timmy stood on his tiptoes to hang a glittery silver ball he'd made in preschool, but he couldn't reach the spot.

"Let me help you." Without missing a beat, Reed lifted Timmy so he could hang the ornament.

Samantha couldn't breathe. This was a scene happening in living rooms across the country, but she couldn't sit back and enjoy it the way she once had. Reed Connors was here, decorating the tree and filling the role of father, the way Art had. She felt as if she were betraying Art by allowing Reed near their son.

The son he hadn't wanted.

Reed raised Timmy higher.

"Be careful," she warned.

Reed's smile faded when he looked at her. "I've got him."

That's what she was afraid of. Reed had no reason to be here. She'd learned at the wedding he was a workaholic bachelor who spent more nights in a hotel than at his own apartment. Not exactly the type of guy who got his kicks decorating the family Christmas tree. Or who would enjoy spending a few extra days in a town like Fernville.

Unless he wanted something. Like Timmy.

But she couldn't imagine Reed wanting his son after all this time. Not with his lifestyle and job. Maybe she was being paranoid. Something totally justifiable when one slip of the tongue could expose the secret she'd kept from Helen and Frank and rip away the only family she and Timmy had. Maybe Reed was curious about his son. But paranoia was like an old friend, as common a companion as the afghan her grandmother had crocheted for her high school graduation present—the last present she'd ever received from her family.

No, there was no need to worry.

He placed Timmy on the ground. "Great job, kiddo."

"No more bare spot, Mom."

"Thanks, honey." But Samantha knew there was a bare spot. Not in the tree, but in her heart. No shiny or shimmering ornament was going to fix it, either. Timmy came close, but not even he had been able to fill it. "This tree is our best yet."

Timmy sighed. "You say that every year."

She ruffled his hair. "And every year it's true."

"What do you think, Mr. Connors?" Timmy asked.

Reed's gaze met hers, and the hardness she'd seen before had disappeared. "It's absolutely beautiful."

"Beautiful," she echoed.

He was talking about the tree, but for a moment it seemed as if he meant her. Until he'd returned from college for spring break, she hadn't known he was capable of saying anything remotely romantic and when he had it blew her away. But today it shouldn't mean anything. Samantha hated that it had. She swallowed around the poinsettia-size lump in her throat.

"I chopped down the tree with my grandpa," Timmy said.

Samantha had forgotten she and Reed weren't alone. Not a good thing. In fact it was a very bad thing. Timmy was the most important thing in her life. She bit the inside of her cheek.

"Do you cut a tree every year?" Reed asked.

Timmy nodded. "My dad used to come with us."

The light in her son's eyes dimmed, and a pain stabbed Samantha's heart. Timmy missed Art so much, and nothing she did seemed to make it better. She tried to fulfill both roles, but her son needed a father or at least a male figure in his life besides his grandfather. So far her attempts to find one had failed. Dating just wasn't her thing.

"I'm sure he was with you when you cut down the tree," Reed said matter-of-factly before she could comfort her son. "I bet he watches when you play ball."

Timmy's eyes filled with hope. "Really?"

"Really," Reed repeated with confidence. He handed the

final ornament to Timmy. "Why don't you put the last one on?"

A smile returned to Timmy's face. Gratitude was the last thing she ever wanted to feel toward Reed Connors, but she couldn't help herself. Back in high school he never knew the right things to say, but just now he had and had made a difference to her son. She caught Reed's attention and mouthed the words "thank you." He shrugged as if it were nothing. But it was something. Something important for Timmy. Maybe Reed did care about his son. Better late than never. Or was it?

Reed was correct. Art was still with them. It didn't matter if he wasn't present physically. He was here in every other way. He had done so much for her and Timmy when he was alive. If only she had loved him more than she had....

Reed held up a box. "Tinsel time."

She remembered the first time Timmy had put tinsel on the tree when he was three. The tree had resembled a crinkled piece of aluminum foil. "Don't forget, the tinsel goes on—"

"One strand at a time," both Timmy and Reed said at the same time and laughed.

"How did you know that?" Timmy asked him.

"My mother used to tell me the same thing," Reed admitted.

"Smart woman," Samantha said.

"Yes, she is." Reed looked at Timmy. "The older I get, the smarter she gets."

"My mom's already smart."

At least someone thought so. And an important someone at that. She smiled. "You're a smart kid for realizing that."

The decorating continued—one strand at a time. With Reed's help, Timmy placed the angel on the top of the tree. Samantha plugged in the multicolored lights. The tree sparkled and twinkled and shone.

"Pizza time," Timmy announced.

"Thanks, but I need to be going." Reed's voice sounded strained.

Timmy groaned. "But we always have pizza after finishing the tree."

"Timmy," Samantha cautioned, though Reed's wanting to leave so suddenly seemed a little strange to her. Maybe he had plans tonight.

"It was nice of you to visit, Mr. Connors," Timmy said, more than a little annoyed. "Thanks for the help."

"Thanks for inviting me." Reed shook Timmy's hand, but withdrew his quickly. "I had fun."

Samantha wanted him gone before Timmy invited Reed to anything else. Today had been enough. She grabbed his coat from the shaker-peg wall rack by the front door and handed it to him. His gaze lingered on Timmy. Too long for her comfort level.

She opened the door. "Goodbye, Reed."

"Good night," he said through tight lips.

She stood on the porch and watched him walk to his rental car. An overwhelming sense of relief washed over her. Reed Connors was leaving. She straightened the red ribbon on the pine wreath hanging on her front door.

Timmy raced outside. "When are you going home?"

"Not for a few days," Reed answered.

Timmy's bright grin could light up the display of Christmas lights in the town square. "Cool."

Cool for him, but not for her. What could possibly keep Reed Connors in Fernville for a few more days?

Chapter Four

Monday morning Reed found himself outside Samantha's flower shop once again, but it wasn't the same as yesterday. Everything had changed in the past twenty-four hours. Anger and frustration pulsed through his veins. He needed answers. An explanation to help him make sense of what he'd figured out. A reason to tell him why he shouldn't hate Samantha.

Reed stared at the color printout of his second-grade school photo his mother had scanned and e-mailed this morning and he'd printed at Patrick's. Reed and Timmy could be twins.

Would Samantha tell him the truth? Reed was about to find out. As he opened the door, a bell jingled. He stepped inside, his stomach tied up in double knots.

A woman in her early twenties stood behind the counter. Her hair was a mass of brown curls barely contained by a headband with two bobbing antlers on top. She wore a red and green apron and greeted him with a smile. "Can I help you?"

Reed removed his gloves and shoved them into his jacket pocket. "Is Samantha here?"

"She's working in her office."

"I'm an old friend of hers from high school." Reed flashed her his most charming smile. The one that usually got him what he wanted. "Would you mind if I went in to see her?"

"Uh, sure. Go ahead." The woman motioned to the doorway behind her. "Into the workroom. The office is on the left."

"Thanks." Reed walked into a room with a large table in the center. Shelves full of ribbon spools and every type of vase imaginable covered the walls. Large white buckets contained colorful flowers. So many stems Reed wondered how many they had to throw away each day. Not exactly cost effective. Two doors were on the left wall of the room. One said Restroom. He knocked on the other.

"Come in," Samantha called out.

Reed took a deep breath, opened the door and froze. He'd expected an orderly office similar to her tidy cottage, not the mess in front of him. A photograph of Timmy in a baseball uniform held a place of honor on top of a file cabinet—the only flat surface not stacked with catalogs and papers. Yellow Post-it notes were stuck everywhere. A calendar with a picture of a Christmas centerpiece hung on the wall above a computer that sat on a dinged, gray metal desk. With a buzzing fluorescent light and no windows, the office was a far cry from his office, a far cry from anything professional. He shouldn't have been surprised based on what her locker had looked like in high school.

She typed on her computer keyboard. A single braid hung down her back. "Don't tell me, Ginny, Mr. Krauss wants the bouquet delivered today not tomorrow and wants black orchids to go in it," Samantha said without turning around.

"Guess again."

As she turned in her chair, Samantha knocked a stack of papers off the desk. She kneeled to pick them up off the floor, and Reed did the same. He handed her a pile of invoices. His fingers brushed hers. Tingles raced up the length of his arm. Once upon a time, the reaction would have meant something to him, but now it was only a distraction to what he needed to do.

"We have to talk," he said.

She said nothing, but the mixture of emotion in her eyes—fear, wariness, anger—spoke volumes. She'd better be prepared to say something, because he wanted answers and he wanted them now.

Samantha pursed her lips. Once Reed would have thought that meant she wanted a kiss. Now it looked as if she was pouting.

"About Timmy," Reed added.

He watched for a reaction. He didn't get one. She'd become a better actress over the years. Or maybe she'd always been this good at hiding the truth. She sure had fooled him.

"Close the door."

He did and sat on a chair needing to be reupholstered or thrown out. It didn't take his M.B.A. to know she was struggling financially like small business owners across the country.

Samantha clasped her hands and placed them on her lap. Always the princess even though she no longer lived in the tower. It was time she was knocked off her throne.

"Timmy's my son."

"He's *my* son." Her voice never wavered. "And Art's."

Reed had wanted—hoped—she would tell him the truth as soon as he asked, but that wasn't going to happen. He really hadn't known her at all. The realization tore at his insides.

"I want to know everything."

Leaning back in her chair, she furrowed her brows. "Where would you like me to start? His conception or his birth?"

How could Reed have ever thought she was perfect, his ideal woman when he was younger? Anger raged within him. "Did Art know you'd gone straight from my bed to his? One minute a virgin, the next a slut?"

Though Reed had no proof she hadn't been a virgin, he realized now she had only told him that, and he'd stupidly believed her. He'd been too inexperienced about women back then to know for sure.

Samantha didn't flinch, but hurt flashed in her eyes. Reed was past the point of caring.

"Of course, Art knew everything that happened between you and me." She spoke with a hint of impatience.

Reed tossed the picture of himself at her. A picture proving everything. "Did Art know I was Timmy's father?"

She glanced at the photo. "That's not funny."

"You'd better believe it's not funny." Anger surged. Reed gritted his teeth. "I can't believe you kept this a secret from me for all these years. Do you know how it feels to find out you have a son you knew nothing about?"

Her startled gaze met his. "Y-you knew."

"I didn't know anything." His temper spiraled out of control. He struggled to remain calm and forced himself to remain seated. "Not until I met Timmy yesterday."

"B-but Art told you I was pregnant."

Reed stared blankly at her. "No, he didn't."

"Yes, he did." She choked the words out. "We skipped school. I went with him to Boston. I stayed outside while he went up to your room and told you everything." Her bottom lip quivered. "I know Art told you about the baby. About Timmy."

"So I am his father."

Her gaze held his for what seemed forever. She nodded.

It was true. Reed was a father, and he had a son. Timmy. Reed sat stunned. A child. His child.

"You knew." She kept repeating the words over and over, but she began to look panicked. "You had to know."

As reality sank in, raw pain sliced through him. He had an almost eight-year-old son. Reed had missed out on so much. Shock gave way to more anger.

"This doesn't make any sense." As she straightened the stack of invoices that were already perfectly aligned, her hands shook. "Art told me… He wouldn't lie."

Reed didn't know if she was the one lying, the one capable of such deception, but he believed Art Wilson was capable of anything. "Why didn't you tell me you were pregnant?"

"I…I wanted to, but I couldn't. Everything was crazy. Out of control. I was so nervous." Her tone was strained. Her breathing ragged. She crossed her arms over her chest and rubbed her upper arms. "Art offered to do it, and I let him."

Reed wasn't sure if he wanted to hear the answer, but he had to ask the question. "What did Art tell you?" The steadiness of Reed's voice surprised him, especially with the war raging inside him.

"He said you were surprised to see him. That he told you about my pregnancy, that you were the father and I needed you back in Fernville. Then he—" Her voice cracked. Tears glistened. She glanced up at the ceiling and took a deep breath. As she exhaled, her shoulders slumped. She stared at the graying linoleum. "Then Art said that you said you were sorry but you had your own life to live. A wife and baby weren't part of it. You didn't want us. You didn't want anything to do with our baby."

A tense silence enveloped the confines of the small room. If she was telling the truth, Art's deception had to be as big a shock to her as Reed discovering he was a father. "I never spoke with Art in Boston. Hell, I didn't know he was ever there. I didn't know about the baby."

"I don't believe you."

Not even the best actress could fake the conviction in her voice. Her utter disbelief in him shook Reed to his core. All these years, Samantha had believed he'd known about their baby and done nothing. The realization pressed down on his chest like a two-ton weight. He struggled to breathe. "It's the truth."

"No." Her gaze pinned him, pleaded with him. Her face paled. "Art wouldn't have lied to me. He was a good man." The words tumbled from her lips. "He's the one who suggested we get married even though he knew the baby wasn't his. He's the one who suggested he raise Timmy as his own son. He's the one who turned down a baseball scholarship to play minor league ball, then blew out his arm that first season. He's the one who gave up everything, including his dreams, for Timmy and me."

Jealousy stirred in Reed. He was the one who should have done that. Reed had never hated anyone as much as he hated Art Wilson. "What else did Art say?"

"On the way home that night, he told me everyone makes mistakes, and his was breaking up with me. He wasn't about to let me go again. He loved me and knew he wanted to spend the rest of his life with me and have a family. Knowing the baby was mine was enough for him. He said marriage was the best option for everyone involved."

Reed wanted to say so much, but he couldn't. Not when the pain was so raw. "I swear to you. I didn't know about Timmy."

She clutched the arm of her chair and choked out a "No."

As realization sank in, the play of emotion on her face

eared Reed's heart. "I would have never walked out on
ny child."

Her gaze flew to his. "You walked out on me."

Reed remembered the heartbreak, the hurt, the betrayal
er four words—*Art wants me back*—had brought with
1em. Reed knew he hadn't stood a chance, and she had
nly been using him to get her ex-boyfriend back, so he'd
eft without fighting for what he wanted. Slunk away was
more apt description if he were being honest. His tight
nuscles tensed even more. "You chose Art."

She huddled in her chair. "There was never a choice to
nake."

Reed had always known the truth, but to hear it from her
ps... Her words were like arrows to his heart.

"Over eight years and you never contacted me." Two
nes formed over the bridge of her nose. The same as they
ad on Timmy. Her son. His son. Their son. "Did you ever
onsider there might have been a consequence to our night
ogether?"

"We used protection." Reed's response had been auto-
natic. An excuse, he realized, more than a reason. He'd
een too heartbroken to think of anything but how she'd
urt him. He'd never thought how it might affect her. Never
onsidered pregnancy and a baby once. Shame and regret
tabbed at him.

"Only abstinence is foolproof. Someone as smart as you
hould know that."

The depth of emotion in her eyes made Reed lean back
gainst the couch. He'd never seen her so serious or upset.
"If you had told me—"

"If you had found out I was pregnant, what would you
ave done? Given up your scholarship to Boston College
nd come back to Fernville to marry me? You had big
reams. Dreams you're living. Would you have given them
ll up?"

"I would never have walked out on my own child," Reed said. "I would have worked something out. Done the right thing."

Her eyes clouded. Once again she didn't believe him.

Damn. Reed brushed his hand through his hair. "Now that I know the truth, things will be different."

She eyed him warily. "Different how?"

"Tell me what you need—financially, emotionally, whatever it takes to do right by our son. I'm Timmy's father."

"Everyone, including Timmy, thinks Art is his father." She wet her lips. "It's even on his birth certificate."

"Art is gone." And rotting in some corner of Hell if there was any justice in the universe, Reed thought. "Timmy needs a father. He needs me."

"Timmy doesn't know you."

"We'll have to remedy that. As soon as possible."

"No."

The panic on her face almost made him feel sorry for her. *Almost* being the operative word. He didn't understand why she was against this. Against him. They had both made mistakes in the past. Big ones. But they had their son's future to consider.

"I've missed the first eight years of my son's life," Reed explained. "Not just me, but my entire family."

Reed couldn't imagine how this would affect his parents once they found out the truth. They had four granddaughters who they spoiled and doted upon. Timmy would be their first grandson, and the oldest of all the grandchildren.

"Timmy has family." Samantha wrung her hands together. "The Wilsons *are* his grandparents. They have no idea Art wasn't Timmy's father."

"You have to tell them the truth." Art's parents weren't really Timmy's grandparents. Not like Reed's parents would be.

"I can't tell them. It would devastate them." Tears immed in Samantha's eyes. "Frank has a heart condi-on."

"You can't keep Timmy from me." Reed thought about s relationship with his own father. He wasn't about to let e past repeat itself with him and Timmy. "I have rights. ights I'll pursue in court."

"Are you threatening me?"

"I won't allow you to keep my son from me and my mily."

Her gaze locked with his. No one moved. No one said aything. The only noise came from the lights overhead. ven the computer hard drive sounded eerily silent. So this as what they'd come to—the threat of legal action to see s son.

It might have been a century since they spoke of their ve and had made love. They weren't childhood sweet-earts. They weren't reunited lovers. They were simply two rangers who shared the most important thing in the orld—a child.

"What do you want?" Samantha's voice sounded re-gned.

"I want to spend time with Timmy. Get to know him."

Her forehead wrinkled. "He's in school during the day."

"The afternoons will be fine."

"And then?" she asked.

"I go back to Boston this weekend and we'll have to e."

She blinked. Once. Twice. Reed was sure she was going cry, but she managed to hold herself together. "You can e Timmy as much as you want until you leave, but only you promise not to tell anyone why you're spending time gether."

"I agree," Reed said. "But only until the end of the eek."

*   *   *

Even before Reed left her office, Samantha had start
trembling. Now that he was gone, it had gotten worse. S
stared at the computer monitor, but the image blurred wi
the tears.

She had only been trying to do the right thing. How ha
it turned out so wrong?

When she had found out she was pregnant, Samanth
had wanted to tell Reed. Whether he loved her or not,
was the father of her child and deserved to know the trut
But it hadn't been easy for her to do. A letter seemed to
impersonal, a phone call too casual. She decided to tell h
parents instead, but that had turned into a living nightmar
She finally turned to Art, who had asked her to the seni
formal. She never expected him to stand by her, but he ha
and had taken her to Boston to tell Reed about the baby
person. But she'd been too scared to face him, so Art ha
offered to do it for her.

If only she had done it herself….

What had Art been thinking? Everything he had don
from proposing marriage to raising Timmy as his own so
showed Samantha how much Art had cared about he
Loved her. Unless all his sacrifices had been due to gui
over what he'd done—or rather failed to do. The thoug
squeezed her heart.

She was so confused at this point. She didn't know wh
to believe. In only a few hours Reed would be back to se
Timmy.

What if Reed wanted Timmy? Not just in the afternoo
for a week, but always? And what if he followed throug
with what he had threatened—a lawsuit?

Samantha wished she could say Reed wasn't capable
something so horrible, but she never really knew him. N
the way she thought she had. Though she had been rig
about his not wanting her, she'd been wrong about his n

vanting Timmy. Dead wrong. A surge of guilt was quickly
eplaced by fear.

She didn't know much about the software industry, but
 vice president title probably brought a high-paying salary
vith it. Reed's clothing and shoes told her he didn't shop
.t thrift or discount stores like she did. Not to mention
Boston wasn't a cheap town to live in. He could afford the
•est child-custody lawyers money could buy. Unlike her.
She had trouble making the monthly lease on the flower
hop and lived in a cottage on the edge of the Wilsons'
•roperty. No way could she afford to fight Reed in court.
Dread shivered down her spine.

No way could she lose her son.

Would it come to that? Would Reed take Timmy from
er?

That afternoon Samantha stared into her office at Reed
nd Timmy playing a computer game on Reed's laptop.
Seeing the two of them together was strange, disconcerting,
rightening. The two looked so comfortable sitting next to
ach other. As if that was how it was supposed to be.

"What do you like to eat?" Reed asked.

"Candy," Timmy answered.

"What do you usually do after school?"

"Go to my grandparents'."

Reed was asking so many questions. Trying to get to
now Timmy or discover evidence? Samantha clenched her
ist. Something bent in her palm. She glanced at the man-
;led rose stem. Just great, she'd become an eavesdropper
nd was ruining her inventory.

Thank you very much, Reed Connors.

But this was nothing compared to what she'd done to
im. Sure, it hadn't been all her fault, but she took the
•lame. She'd stolen his son. She only hoped he didn't want
im back.

She picked up a pink rose and stuck it into the new baby-girl bouquet she was arranging for the Neil family.

"Don't forget that's a flower stem you're sticking in, no a metal rod." Ginny smiled from the doorway to the store "Not that I blame you for being a little preoccupied."

Preoccupied? Samantha had been on the verge of losin it ever since Reed had shown up this morning, but she ha to keep herself together. She couldn't play into his hand: Not when the stakes were so high.

"I don't know how you do it," Ginny said.

"Do what?"

"Attract men like bees to flowers." Ginny handed he three stems of lavender daisies. "You were married to th best-looking man in town and now you have a Brook Brothers hottie after you."

Reed Connors a hottie? Samantha didn't think so unles one was attracted to the devil. A devil after her son. Sh shoved the daisies into the cradle-shaped basket. "I ca assure you, Reed is not after me."

"The way to a woman's heart is through her kids."

She stuck stems of montecasino with their small pin blooms into the arrangement. Maybe she should add a cou ple white ones, too. "I thought that was with flowers, choc olates and diamonds."

"Just go with me on this, okay?"

"Okay, but you're wrong."

"I don't think so." Ginny rearranged one of the blu irises. "He's definitely interested."

"You've been watching too many chick flicks and read ing too many novels."

"Then why is he here?"

That was the one question Samantha never wanted t answer. "We're…" Enemies, adversaries, ex-lovers. On thing for certain—they weren't friends. She put back a pin tulip. There were already six of them in the bouque

"We're old classmates. He used to tutor me in math and science classes."

"I would have flunked every subject if I could have had a tutor like him."

Samantha adjusted the three pink roses. "You were an honors student."

"I could have faked it." Ginny sighed. "Look at the guy. All that thick, dark hair to run your fingers through. And those eyes. Chocolate brown that makes me want to melt right into his big, strong hands. And that dimpled smile is so sweet. Not to mention the rest of him. Personally I'd love to see what's underneath his navy slacks and oxford shirt. Bet he looks great in a tux. Or out of it."

Samantha had seen the college-boy Reed, but the improved physique of the businessman Reed? Even she understood Ginny's desire. Samantha froze.

What was she thinking? Doing?

Clearly both she and Ginny had lost it. Big-time.

The only place he would make Samantha feel hot was under the collar. He was nothing but a thorn that needed to be pruned out of her life. But because of Timmy, Reed might become a fixture in her life. She didn't know what his involvement would be. Maybe none. No, she wasn't that lucky.

"Hubba, hubba," Ginny said.

"When was the last time you had a date?" Samantha asked.

"When my husband proposed. Two and a half years ago."

Timmy's giggles drifted from the office, and Samantha felt more at ease. She wanted to fill his life with love and laughter. So far it hadn't been easy to do. Not when he missed Art the way he did. And if Reed Connors were suddenly hanging around, it would only get harder.

Ginny pursed her lips. "Even Timmy likes him. Kids are great judges of character."

Timmy did seem to like Reed. Samantha wondered what that meant in the long term. Reed was good at breaking hearts. She didn't want Timmy to get hurt.

"Earth to Samantha," Ginny said.

Samantha's cheeks warmed. She shoved a woody stem of salal into the bouquet. More stems of the grass-green leafy accent were needed to balance all the pink. "Sorry, what did you say?"

"Doesn't matter." Ginny grinned, obviously misreading the reason for her hesitation. "I think I know the answer now."

Before Samantha could question her assistant, Timmy bounced out of her office followed by Reed. "Can we get a milkshake?"

Unease inched down Samantha's spine. Allowing Reed to spend time with Timmy when she was around was one thing, but alone? Too soon. "It's freezing outside and you want a milkshake?"

Timmy rolled his eyes. "We'll be inside where it's warm."

"I—"

"If you'd feel more comfortable—" Reed cocked a brow "—you can chaperone us."

That's what she wanted to do. She didn't trust him. Not with her son.

"It'll be fun, Mom."

Spending time with Reed would be punishment for past deeds, not fun. And in a way she deserved it for being such a chicken and having Art do her dirty work—or rather pretend to do it. If she could change one thing in her life... No, she needed to change about five things. All but one involved Reed.

"Don't forget, you skipped lunch today to make Mrs.

Flynn's get-well bouquet.'' Ginny's eyes twinkled with mischief. "You must be hungry."

Samantha was hungry. Starving to be exact. But eating with Reed Connors wasn't going to do much for her appetite. Not when being near him stressed her out so much she couldn't think straight.

"Come on, Mom," Timmy urged.

She weighed the pros and the cons. The cons definitely had the advantage, but she had to find out what Reed was up to. Samantha would not take anything he said at face value. She'd been naive once, but she wouldn't be taken in again.

"Okay." She washed and dried her hands. "But we don't have all afternoon. I need to finish this bouquet and arrange Mr. Akers's anniversary present for his wife."

"Take your time," Ginny said. "It's slow today so I can do them for you."

"But Mr. Akers—"

"Wanted stargazer lilies and cushion chrysanthemums, right?" Ginny's smile resembled the Cheshire cat's grin. "I can do that."

"Then it's settled," Reed said.

Nothing was settled. And it wouldn't be as long as he was in Fernville and a part of her and Timmy's life.

Chapter Five

The Fernville Creamery was crowded when Reed opened the door for Samantha and Timmy. Kids of all ages crammed into red vinyl booths and not one seat remained at the fountain counter. The noise from at least twenty different conversations battled with the music playing on the old-fashioned juke box for dominance.

It was as if Reed had traveled back in time. Same black-and-white square tile floor. Same chrome fixtures. Same neon red clock. Same scent of frying oil in the air. Nothing had changed since the last time he'd been here except the clothes and hairstyles the customers wore.

"I see a place." Timmy ran ahead.

Strike that. Something had changed. Reed wasn't here with his gang of computer-geek, game-enthusiast, science-fiction-loving friends no one else wanted to sit with or acknowledge. He was here with Samantha and her son.

His son.

Reed still couldn't believe it. He was a father.

The thought made him a little lightheaded. *Overwhelm-*

ing didn't begin to describe how his mind had been spinning like a gyroscope since this morning. He'd tried to return to his room and work, but that had been impossible. So had sleep.

Food would help. As would counseling. The last thing he ever thought he'd have—ever wanted—was a child. And now that he had one, Reed wasn't sure what he was going to do.

He lost sight of Timmy for a moment and glanced at Samantha, wondering if it was okay for Timmy to be so far away from them. She didn't seem concerned so Reed figured it was okay. Parenting was a huge unknown to him.

Playing computer games with Timmy for an hour or so was one thing, but Reed didn't know what to do or where to start when it came to being a dad. His own father hadn't been around enough to be a role model. His two sisters might shove one of his baby nieces into his arms, but neither had ever asked him to baby-sit. They knew better. Yet now he had a son.

Give Reed a new software package and he could take care of marketing that just fine. That was his kind of baby.

But a kid?

He was in over his head. Way over his head.

Reed tried to recall how his dad had acted when they went to a restaurant, but he only had recent memories. None from when he was a kid. That didn't surprise Reed. It had taken an assignment and move to Fernville before Reed had gotten to know his father, but by then he was in high school. A little too late to help him now.

Was it too late for Reed and Timmy?

Reed hoped not. But he lived in Boston and had a job like his father's old one that required lots of travel. Toss in the strained relationship between him and Samantha and it didn't make for an easy road ahead. And easy was all Reed's busy life could handle. He breathed deeply to calm his swirling doubts. He couldn't think about tomorrow, let alone the future. He needed to concentrate on one day at a time.

Timmy waved from the only empty booth in the place. Reed's heart filled with pride and doubt at the sight of his son. "Timmy has excellent vision."

"Takes after me," she said.

Reed was near-sighted and had replaced his bottle-thick glasses with contacts his freshman year of college. "Better you than me."

"Shhhh," she whispered. "Someone might hear you."

As if that was the worst thing that could happen after this morning. Reed sighed. "I'll be more careful."

If he'd been more careful, he wouldn't be in this situation to begin with. But kissing Samantha by the lake so many years ago had started a chain of events that no one—especially not a twenty-year-old head over heels in love with what he perceived to be his ideal woman—could stop. Back then Samantha had been ideal, with dreams to make the world better, a body that sent blood rushing where he didn't want it to go and a way of making him feel special when that was the last thing he'd ever felt. Things had sure changed. Such as how she made him feel—like an overripe pear covered with fruit flies she couldn't get rid of. He'd assumed she couldn't ever hurt him again. He'd been wrong. And didn't like it. But Reed wasn't about to go anywhere until he figured out what to do about their son.

With a flip of her braid she made a beeline to the table, and Reed followed her. Samantha slid into the booth next to Timmy.

"Would it be okay if Reed sat next to me?" Timmy asked her.

Timmy's request surprised Reed. The afternoon hadn't gone that well. He'd learned his son was a sports nut. Reed liked sports but wasn't crazy about them like Timmy. Their only common ground had been computer games and J.R.R. Tolkien. Not the best start for a lasting relationship.

Tension etched itself on Samantha's face. In the lines on her forehead. In the tightness of her mouth. But the corners of her mouth edged up, the way they used to, in a perfect rendition of a Mona Lisa smile.

"Not a problem." She moved to the opposite side.

Progress? Maybe a little. Reed wasn't sure if all the progress in the world could make the situation better. A son. He had a feeling this week might feel like a year by the time he returned to Boston. And once he was back home, he couldn't imagine what would happen next.

"Thanks, Mom." As Timmy grinned, his dimple seemed to wink at Reed as he sat. "You're the best."

Reed picked up his menu—nothing more than a laminated piece of paper. "This is the same menu from the last time I was here."

The last time…

It had been that fateful spring break, and he had sat in this same booth. He'd forgotten until that moment, but now it seemed like yesterday. Reed remembered walking in with Samantha for a milkshake and all the kids staring at them. In awe or disbelief, it hadn't mattered. She was so beautiful and with him. Art and his cronies had been sitting in a booth near the front, and for a moment Reed thought he was a dead man but he hadn't cared. For the first time in his life, he'd felt like the king of the world, and it was worth dying for with Samantha by his side.

But she was no longer by his side or on it. Truth be told, she had never been and never would be. The realization brought a bittersweet disappointment that surprised him.

But he couldn't pretend that what they'd shared in the past hadn't mattered to him, that what he'd felt for her hadn't been real, that she hadn't stolen his heart. She was the mother of his child and would be a part of his life from here on out.

"My mom and dad came here a lot, did you?" Timmy asked.

"A few times." Reed toyed with the paper napkin he'd placed on his lap. He wished he *could* put the past behind him, but Timmy would be a reminder of it now. "But my friends and I spent more time in the school's computer lab or at each other's houses playing games."

Timmy's mouth formed a perfect O. "So that's why you're so good at them."

His compliment pleased Reed. Maybe he wasn't doing so badly with his son. "I play them when I'm on a long flight. My job takes me all over the world and I always seem to be flying somewhere."

"I've never been on an airplane before, but we're going to go to Walt Disney World," Timmy said. "Aren't we, Mom?"

"Someday." She sounded wistful but looked tense and cautious.

The sparkle and anticipation in Timmy's eyes made Reed want to fulfill the dream. He had built up more frequent flier mileage and hotel awards than he could ever use. Enough for twenty first-class trips to Orlando. What would it be like to take a son to Disney World...? Not that Samantha would let him.

"Why aren't you working today, Mr. Connors?" Timmy asked.

Samantha sucked in a breath. Fear took over her features for a moment, but was soon gone. She didn't trust him, but the feeling was mutual. It still hurt that she hadn't believed in him enough to give him the benefit of the doubt all these years.

"It's been a long time since I've been back in town so I took the week off," Reed explained. "Thought I'd catch up with old friends and see how much Fernville has changed.''

Her gaze met his, and Reed thought he saw relief in Samantha's eyes. He'd said he wouldn't say anything about being Timmy's father, and he wouldn't. But she couldn't expect him to keep the secret forever. That wouldn't be fair to anybody.

Timmy leaned toward him. "You'll be here all week?"

Reed nodded. "Until Sunday."

A smile erupted on Timmy's face. "Cool."

Until that moment Reed hadn't realized how cool it was. Timmy was a great kid. Reed wanted to get to know him better.

Samantha, however, looked anything but happy. Her knotted brows were a dead giveaway. Biology class had given her the same expression. Just great. He ranked up there with dead frogs, photosynthesis and the smell of formaldehyde.

She placed her menu behind the napkin dispenser. "I'm ready to order."

"I know what you want, Mom." Timmy pretended to take her order. "French fries and a chocolate malt."

"That's right," she said.

"She always orders the same thing."

Her smile directed at Timmy reminded Reed when she had once looked lovingly at him. That wasn't going to happen again. Disappointment shot through him, and he ignored it.

She narrowed her eyes. "I happen to like the same thing—"

"Me, too," Timmy said. "I want a half-and-half milkshake."

Reed studied the menu. "I don't see that one."

"It's not, but they'll make it for me," Timmy explained.

"It was my dad's favorite. Half vanilla and half chocolate."

The enthusiasm in Timmy's voice faded, and Reed knew why. Timmy missed Art. Three years wasn't a long time, and Timmy had been old enough to have memories of the man he called dad. Reed had spent years perfecting the right words to say in any situation, but he felt out of his element here. He fought the urge to build a tower out of the packs of sugar on the table like he and his friends did when they came here.

Samantha, however, knew what to do. She reached across the table and squeezed Timmy's hand. The look of tenderness in her eyes as she stared at her son brought a lump to Reed's throat. She loved her son with every ounce of her being. That much was clear. And it made all the difference to Timmy.

"You should try one," Timmy suggested. "It's really good."

Reed was tempted but didn't think it was a good idea today. He didn't want to be cruel. "Sounds tasty, but I'm going to order my favorite, a vanilla shake."

"My dad sometimes ordered those, too." Timmy scooted toward Reed. "Didn't he, Mom?"

"Yes, he did, honey." Her voice softened to almost a caress, the same tone she'd once used to whisper "I love you" to Reed. He pushed the memory aside. All he wanted to hear now was an "I like you." He'd settle for an "I'll tolerate you." Anything to make it easier to get to know his son.

"I thought I remembered that." Timmy smiled at Reed. "You and my dad have something in common, Mr. Connors."

More than you can imagine, kid. "Why don't you call me Reed? Mr. Connors makes me sound like a teacher."

"Or old," Timmy said.

Reed laughed. "Out of the mouths of babes."

Timmy frowned. "I'm not a baby. I'm almost eight."

"It's just a saying that's been around forever," Reed explained.

"You still called me a baby." Those two familiar lines formed above Timmy's nose. "No, a babe. Didn't he, Mom?"

"Well—" Samantha's smile reached her eyes and took Reed's breath away the way it used to "—if you want to get technical, sweetie, yes, he did."

He frowned both at the effect she had on him and how she was against him in front of their son. A united front was better. That was one thing Reed remembered from his father. His dad might have been away, but he always took Reed's mother's side and supported her. Would that ever be the case with him and Samantha?

"I didn't mean—"

"But you said it," Timmy said.

"Yes, I did." Reed felt as if he had been cornered by a Fortune 500 information system's manager who had found a bug in Wintersoft's latest software release that made it incompatible with every platform on the market. But this situation with Timmy wasn't *that* big a problem. Reasoning with a kid had to be easier than dealing with irate engineers, programmers and managers. "The saying 'out of the mouths of babes' means children speak the truth without worrying about the consequences."

Timmy stared at him. Samantha, too.

"It's cute…no, not cute. It's funny what kids say," Reed tried again. "Funny ha-ha, not funny strange."

"I'm not strange," Timmy said. "Am I mom?"

Samantha pressed her lips together. It looked as if she was about to burst out laughing. For the first time all day, she was enjoying herself. Figures it would be at Reed's expense. Just as it had been when he was in high school.

Nerds R Us. But Samantha had acted as if she understood how he felt and never put him down. Even stood up for him once or twice. If only it were the same now.... Reed picked up a white sugar package.

"Not at all, honey," she said, her tone full of amusement.

Timmy's relief made Reed feel worse. Timmy stuck out his bottom lip. "And I'm not a babe, either."

"No, you're not." Okay, maybe reasoning wasn't the way to go. Reed brushed his hand through his hair. "I'm sorry for bringing it up."

"That's okay. I forgive you." Timmy spun the salt shaker around in its chrome holder. "But don't do it again."

"I won't." Dealing with Nate Leeman's team of programmers and software engineers was much easier than dealing with an eight-year-old boy. Reed had a lot to learn about being a dad.

"Can I call you Reed instead of Mr. Connors?" Timmy asked.

"If it's okay with your mom." Reed realized he should have mentioned that caveat when he first mentioned it. Upsetting Samantha would make the situation worse. Though he couldn't imagine anything worse than it already was.

Timmy leaned over the table toward her. "Mom?"

"It's okay." Samantha boldly met Reed's gaze. "We wouldn't want Mr. Connors to feel old, now would we?"

Forget about feeling old. Reed had never felt so inexperienced and immature. His first outing as a father and he'd failed miserably. He only hoped to do better tomorrow.

That evening Samantha sat on the floor of her living room surrounded by wrapping paper, ribbon and presents. The lights on the tree provided a festive glow. The spinning windmill in the snow globe created a miniblizzard inside. Carols filled the room with holiday cheer. But she didn't feel like singing along. She didn't even feel like smiling. The spirit of Christmas was missing. It was the eighth of December but it might as well have been July.

Samantha tied a candy cane and a small, leather baseball mitt ornament to one of Timmy's Christmas presents. She added a red bow. Santa or his elves couldn't have done better. So why did she feel like a total failure? As a mother, a wife, a woman.

She reached for the next gift—a cookbook for her mother-in-law—and forced herself to hum along to "Deck The Halls." Too bad she knew where she wanted to shove the boughs of holly.

Don't think about him.

She'd wasted too much time and energy thinking about Reed Connors.

She stared at the snow globe. Santa had disappeared under a snowdrift. If only this day could vanish, too. She didn't want to think about this morning. It hurt too bad. Always would.

The telephone rang. She glanced at the clock she'd hung on the wall yesterday that played a different Christmas carol on each hour. Almost nine-thirty. Too late for telemarketers. Her friends rarely called past nine. Reaching for the cordless receiver, she hoped nothing was wrong. "Hello."

"It's Reed."

At the sound of his deep voice, her stomach sprang into back flips. Even with all that had happened, something about him sent a ripple of awareness through her. The man wanted her son, yet she was attracted to him. Talk about certifiable.

She clutched the receiver, uncertain what to say next.

Hanging up seemed like a good option. Saying he'd reached a wrong number did, too.

"Samantha."

"I'm here." Her voice rose an octave. She fought for control against the emotions raging inside her. Fear, anger, frustration, stress. But she couldn't lose it. She had to keep herself together for Timmy's sake. "What do you want?"

"I wanted to thank you for today and let you know I plan to see Timmy again tomorrow."

She remembered when he had last called her and said he couldn't wait to see her. That had been the day before they'd made love, two days before her life had fallen apart.

"I said you could see him while you were in town."

"I wanted to make sure." He paused. "Things, plans change."

Samantha's senses went on alert. Reed had always been polite, but he seemed to be up to something. And that worried her. She knew what Reed Connors was capable of— both good and bad. She had to protect her son at all costs. She had to keep Timmy from being hurt or worse, losing him all together.

She shuddered at the thought. "What did you have in mind?"

"I thought I'd leave it to you."

Wrong call. Left to her, Reed would leave Fernville and never come back. He would never spend another second with Timmy. Or her. She remembered a time when she never wanted Reed to leave her and return to college. They had seemed to share everything—their dreams, their love, their souls. Now all they shared was Timmy. She exhaled slowly. "Why is that?"

"You know him. I don't." Reed sounded sincere. "Let's be honest, Sam. The only time I'm around kids is if they happen to be on the same flight as me. And then I hope they don't spend the entire time kicking the back of my seat or crying.''

He was being so open and honest. The way he'd been years ago when he told her that anyone who didn't love her for who she was an idiot. She'd believed him then. Now she knew better. She wouldn't allow herself to be drawn in again. Not when the stakes were so high.

"Do you have any suggestions?" he asked.

Samantha hesitated. She had been trying to rein in her emotions since this morning, but she wasn't doing a good enough job. Reed had threatened to take Timmy. But perhaps anger wasn't the way to approach him.

"Sam?"

"I'm thinking."

Perhaps being polite was the better way to go. It might get her the answers she needed. Or get Reed out of their lives once he got tired of playing Daddy. His lifestyle and job didn't leave room for a son. Make that a long-distance son. If she stuck in there and gave Reed what he wanted—time with Timmy—this might all blow over sooner rather than later.

"You could come over to our house after school," she suggested in a cheerful tone. "If it's nice weather, you can play outside, otherwise we have plenty of stuff to do indoors."

Silence met her suggestion.

She taped the Santa wrapping paper over the cookbook. Not a word. She folded the sides and secured them. Still nothing. A few more seconds of quiet got to her. "Reed? Are you there?

"I'm here," he said finally. "That sounds great."

"Great," she repeated.

"Does three-thirty work for you?"

"Sure." Being polite didn't feel good when he was so appreciative. She felt guilty because she had an ulterior motive and Reed wanted to spend time with her son. "Be warned. Timmy will want to show you everything in his room."

"I can't wait." A beat passed. "And, Samantha. Thanks. I know this isn't easy on you."

The genuine tone of Reed's words carried across the phone line and touched her heart in a way she never would have imagined. But at the same time, it worried her. Immensely.

What exactly did Reed want with Timmy?

Chapter Six

Sitting on the edge of Timmy's bed, Reed placed the bookmark back into the well-worn paperback copy of Tolk-ien's *The Hobbit* and closed the book. "That's all for to-night."

"Just a little more," Timmy said. "Please."

"No more." Reed stood, avoiding the top bunk bed. He didn't know what he was doing when it came to Timmy, but no one seemed to realize it, except him. "Tomorrow's a school day."

Timmy sighed. "You sound like my mom."

Reed took that as a compliment. It was the first time he'd sounded like a parent. Not by much, but it was a start. "Us grown-ups have to stick together."

Today Reed had been more like a wind-up plaything than father figure, spending the afternoon playing cards and board games with Timmy. A means to getting to know his son. That's what all this was about. Reed hoped it was enough.

Things with Samantha had improved, too. She'd invited

him to stay for dinner and allowed him to tuck Timmy into bed. His phone call last night had been a good idea.

"See you tomorrow afternoon, kiddo." Reed stood in the doorway. "Sleep well."

"'Night, Reed."

"Good night."

He turned off the light and closed the door. As he walked down the hallway, he heard Samantha in the kitchen. She had been polite and accommodating today, but he noticed her watchful expression and the way she hovered nearby whenever he was around. Her distrust ran deep.

It had to stop.

For Timmy's sake.

Reed and Samantha had to get along better for things to go smoothly with their son. But in order for that to happen, Reed needed her to agree to put the past behind them and start over with a clean slate. He also needed her to agree to help him. It wasn't going to be easy.

In the kitchen Samantha stood at the sink washing the dishes. She wore her hair loose. The long locks fell to the middle of her back. The same length it had been in high school, but her black turtleneck made her hair look blonder than he remembered.

His footsteps sounded against the tile floor, and Samantha glanced back. "Did you read him an extra chapter?"

"He asked, but I told him it was a school night."

She raised a brow. "And he let you get away with that?"

"Must be because I'm the new guy around."

"That's probably it. Still it's not bad for someone who is only around kids when he's on an airplane."

The compliment sent his confidence soaring since he felt as if he were barely treading water when it came to Timmy.

And Reed was drowning when it came to Samantha. She captivated him. And the way her jeans fit like a second skin and accentuated her long legs and curves...

What the hell was he doing?

This wasn't about her and him. It was about their son. He focused on her eyes. Anything to keep his gaze from traveling downward again.

"It's late." She turned back to the sink and rinsed silverware. "You should get back to town."

He was tired, exhausted from the roller-coaster emotional ride he'd been on since yesterday and from trying to work all morning when his mind was elsewhere. But it wasn't time to call it a night; he and Samantha had things to discuss. Reed wanted to talk about the past, but it wasn't the right time yet. He would start with the present first.

Reed rolled up his sleeves. "After such a delicious dinner, the least I can do is help clean up."

"It's not necessary."

"Yes, it is."

He handed her a dirty plate. She grabbed the opposite edge and they both held on to it. As she stared into his eyes, time seemed to go backward. It was the beginning, the start of their once upon a time as she called his spring break. Reed's heart pounded against his chest.

This was wrong. He shouldn't be thinking this way about her, feeling this nostalgia. But she was more beautiful than ever, and Reed couldn't tear his gaze away from her.

Samantha took the plate from him. "I'm used to doing this myself."

The smart thing would be to leave, but Reed couldn't.

"Everyone can use a little help." He grabbed a dishrag from the countertop and dried a small saucepan. "I could use yours."

She washed the salad bowl. "Why me?"

"Because you don't want anyone to know about me and Timmy. That leaves you to help me."

She squeezed more soap into the bowl. "With what?"

Reed couldn't believe he was about to admit a shortcoming to the one woman who never thought he was good enough to begin with. He placed the saucepan on the counter. "I don't know how to be a parent, a father. My dad wasn't around when I was little so I don't know what to do, how to act, how to parent. I need you to help me learn what I need to know."

"Why should I help you?"

"Because it's what's best for our son."

"Best for him?" She grabbed a sponge and scrubbed the salad bowl. "I suppose you would think taking Timmy away from me is best for him."

"Take Timmy…" Realization hit Reed. Her antagonism. Her fear. Even the sudden change in the polite way she'd treated him today. It all made sense.

"You said you would pursue your rights in court." She threw the sponge into the sink. "That means custody."

Tears flowed down her cheeks. The last time he'd seen her cry, they had been tears of happiness, joy, love. But this time…

Her fear made him realize how much they had hurt each other. Both in the past and present. Reed wiped the tears off her cheek. Her skin was soft under the rough pads of his fingertips. "Don't cry."

She turned her face away from him.

"Look at me, Sam."

Slowly she glanced his way. Even with red-rimmed, teary eyes she was gorgeous. All he wanted to do was hold her in his arms. But he couldn't, could he?

His collar seemed to have shrunk three inches and was strangling him, but this wasn't the time for silence. He cupped her face with his hand, her cheek against his palm. "I see how wonderful you are with Timmy. How much you love him. I would never interfere with that. Not ever."

She tilted her head so he was no longer touching her. "But you said—"

"We both said a lot of things." Reed tossed the dish towel on the counter. "After what Art did—"

"Art must have had a good reason for not telling you." She wet her lips. "But I've been over it a thousand times in my mind and I still can't figure out why he would do something like that. He was a good man."

"I know why," Reed mumbled.

She glanced over at him. "You do?"

"Art loved you, Sam." The words weren't easy for Reed to say because until yesterday he had never believed they were true. But they were. Art had loved Samantha. And she needed to hear that. "That's why he didn't tell me about the baby and told you he had. He loved you so much he didn't want to lose you...to me."

The relief on her face told Reed he'd done the right thing by telling her what he'd figured out.

"But I'd told Art what happened between us." Samantha furrowed her brow. "He knew you didn't care about me. That you didn't fight for me when I told you I was getting back with him. That you left Fernville without a word."

But Reed had cared. Too much. That had been his problem. His stomach knotted, but her sadness made him forget about his own pain. The urge to touch her was strong, but he kept himself from comforting her. Samantha needed to understand the truth more than she needed a shoulder to cry on.

"I left because I was hurt. Not because I didn't care. You wanted Art, not me. I couldn't face it. Or you. So I retreated. Ran away. Immersed myself in college and never looked back."

Samantha started to speak than stopped herself.

"What?" Reed asked.

She hesitated. "Art never wanted me back." She spoke in a broken whisper. "I made that up. I lied. I needed to know you cared about me. And that we…I hadn't made a mistake.''

"Sam—"

"It was immature and childish, a really stupid thing to do.'' She stared at the water in the sink. "But I was ashamed and embarrassed and felt like you'd used me after we'd made love. I'd planned on waiting until I got married. It was one of the reasons Art and I broke up. He wanted to, I didn't. But that spring break you and I spent together…it was magical. I'd never felt anything like it and I didn't want it to end. You were going back to Boston for college and I was going to be in Fernville without you. I got scared and was afraid I'd made a huge mistake. I wanted to know you felt the same way I did, so I told you Art wanted me back to see what you would do. But when you didn't do or say anything, I realized what we had had only been a dream. And it had all been a mistake.''

One mistake on top of another. So much had been lost and for no reason. Reed wanted to kick himself. No, he wanted to go back nine years ago and do it all over again. But that wasn't possible. "I cared, Samantha. I was so crazy about you in high school, I couldn't see straight, but I was only your friend. The nerd who helped you pass your classes. I couldn't compete with the mighty and popular Art Wilson. But when I came home for spring break, everything was different. It was the best week of my life. But when you said Art wanted to get back together, I knew it was over. There was no way you'd want me instead of Mr. Popular All-Star so I ran away with my tail between my legs. It hurt so bad I couldn't come back to Fernville. I'm sorry.''

"Me, too,'' she said softly.

Silence surrounded them. The what-ifs ran through Reed's mind. He wondered if Samantha was thinking the same thing.

Art wasn't responsible for everything that had gone wrong. And that made this hurt all the more. "This wasn't only Art's fault."

She nodded. "We're all to blame."

"Everyone except Timmy."

She raised her gaze to his. "What do you want with Timmy?"

"I don't know," Reed admitted. "The past two days have all been so confusing. I've been trying to figure out what being Timmy's father means and how involved I will be in his life. Or can be, living in Boston. The logistics alone are mind-boggling. But no matter how upset I am for not knowing about my son, I do know my wanting or seeking full custody wouldn't be in Timmy's best interest."

"Do you mean that? Honestly? No games or tricks?"

"No games." Reed took a step closer to her. "We need to figure this out together."

"Together," she whispered.

"That's right. Together. We have to be able to get along." Reed took one of her soapy-water-covered hands in his. He was relieved when she didn't jerk it away. "And I believe for that to happen we need to put the past behind us and start over."

She bit her lip. "That doesn't sound too easy."

"It's not going to be easy, but it's worth a try for our son." Reed realized he was still holding Samantha's hand. She hadn't seemed to notice, either. Until he let go, and her cheeks reddened. "For Timmy?"

She nodded. "For Timmy."

The next afternoon Samantha stared out the window and saw the expression of joy on Timmy's face as he played catch with Reed. This was what her son needed—a male influence in his life—a man besides his grandfather, who was having to take it easier with his heart condition.

If only Samantha had let her occasional dating go past the first or second dates so Timmy would have had other men to play catch and hang out with. But she hadn't. Now she was stuck with Reed and had herself to blame.

No, that wasn't fair.

Reed was Timmy's father. Nothing would change that. But what if Reed had come back to Fernville before now…?

What-might-have-beens weren't going to change anything. They had decided to put the past behind them and get along, and that's what she was trying to do. But she still felt on edge and confused. Overemotional at times.

After Reed and Timmy had finished playing a board game, Samantha had found them going through the scrapbooks. The raw pain in Reed's eyes as he paged through Timmy's life up to his seventh birthday had sent tears streaming down her face.

So many mistakes and misunderstandings. Too many.

But apologies and regrets wouldn't make up for what he'd lost, what he'd missed out on. Nothing would. They had to focus on the most important thing—Timmy—and move forward.

So far Timmy seemed like the only one ready to do that. He had welcomed Reed into his life with open arms. And when he wasn't around, all she heard was Reed this and Reed that. She couldn't get away from it. From him.

Reed was going to be here until Sunday, but it wouldn't be a celebration of relief when he returned to Boston. Timmy was getting attached to him. And in a way, so was she. Having him around wasn't as bad as she thought it would be. Not that she wanted him in Fernville permanently.

Cold air seeped through the single-paned window, and Samantha backed away. She couldn't stand here and stare at them all afternoon. Lately that seemed like all she did.

er gaze rested on a picture of her and Art taken a month
efore his motorcycle accident.

Art had been an excellent father and husband. Everything
e'd done had been for the good of his family. For them.
ut he had taken Timmy from Reed.

She might be angry, but she couldn't hate Art for his lie.
ne mistake didn't erase all the other good things he'd
one for her and Timmy. It didn't erase the love Art had
own her when no one else had.

If only she had been strong enough to tell Reed, but
e'd relied on Art, on his strength instead of her own.

Things would have been so different had she done it
rself. Better? She didn't know. Samantha had loved
eed, but would love have been enough? He was so dif-
rent now. Both of them were. Would those changes have
riven them apart or pulled them together? She would never
ow that answer, either.

With her fingertip, she touched Art's picture. "Reed and
immy. Your parents…it's all so confusing. I wish you
ere here to help me figure it out."

Something hit the side of the house with a loud thud,
d Samantha jumped.

The front door cracked open. "Sorry, Mom. Wild
tch."

With that, Timmy slammed the door and was gone.

She placed her hand over her pounding chest, took a
ep breath and stared at Art's to-die-for smile and the
refree look in his blue eyes. "If that was supposed to be
me sort of sign, it didn't tell me anything."

Samantha almost expected Art to speak or wink or shrug.
ut his image remained frozen, captured in print and un-
anging.

She was on her own. As usual.

But this time felt…different. Samantha had never felt so
rn about what to do. When she'd been in high school and

pregnant, she hadn't needed to make a choice. Art wante
her; Reed hadn't. Or so she'd thought. But now a decisio
several most likely, had to be made.

What did Reed being Timmy's father mean in the lon
term? She wasn't about to erase Art from her and Timmy
memory banks. She couldn't forget about Helen and Fran
and how much they meant to her. She didn't want to los
the family she had, which meant keeping the truth abou
Timmy a secret. But Reed...

What did he deserve?

His son?

Samantha shivered at the thought, despite Reed's claim
of only wanting to get to know Timmy. But her fear wasn
as strong as it had once been. She recognized a chink i
Reed Connors's armor. His lack of confidence in his abilit
to be a good father made him vulnerable. It would be s
easy to take advantage of that, but she couldn't. Not whe
she hadn't forgotten the boy he'd once been. His vulnera
bility reminded her of the Reed she'd admired and loved
A stark contrast to the hard edge, to the drive and the pas
sion she saw in him now.

But no matter how vulnerable he appeared she couldn
allow herself to fall for the new and improved Reed Cor
nors. No matter how charming and handsome he'd become
No matter how much he might think he needed her help.

Samantha wasn't stupid.

It didn't matter that Reed had told her last night he'
cared about her back then. Whatever his feelings had beer
they hadn't been enough. He had stayed away from her fo
years. Timmy was the reason Reed was back in her life
Nothing was going to change that. Not that she wanted
to change, she reminded herself. Reed hadn't loved her be
fore, and she wouldn't ever give him another chance to hu
her again.

Not even for Timmy's sake.

* * *

Snow flurries floated down from the darkening sky, but
ed wasn't ready to call it quits. Timmy tossed him the
ll and it hit Reed's mitt—one he'd bought at the sporting
ods store this morning—with a thwack.

Playing catch with his son. It didn't get much better than
s. He threw the ball back, making Timmy reach for it.
e kid caught it, no problem. Pride filled Reed at his son's
letic abilities. He must get that from Samantha or maybe
was some latent gene that had missed him. "Good
tch."

Timmy beamed. "Do you like to go to the movies and
t popcorn and candy?"

More questions. Reed smiled. Timmy had been asking
m questions all afternoon. Either the kid was curious, or
wanted to be a reporter when he got older and was
ning his interviewing skills. "Yes to all three. But I don't
ve a lot of spare time to go to the movies."

"Because of work?"

Reed nodded. The kid was sharp. "I want to do the best
o I can and sometimes it takes a lot of time."

"Kinda like me wanting to be the best pitcher I can be.
kes practice and hard work."

"Exactly." Reed reached for the ball and barely caught
"Watch that arm of yours or you'll hit the house again."

Timmy shrugged. "My mom doesn't mind."

Somehow Reed doubted that. Samantha had opinions on
erything. Still, his respect for her was growing. Running
usiness while raising a son on her own couldn't be easy.
it Samantha was doing it and doing it well. He saw that
e struggled financially. Somehow he would have to
oach the subject of child support. What he lacked in free
ne, he could easily make up for monetarily.

The ball sailed back and forth. The temperature dropped,

turning Timmy's cheeks and nose red. A few more minut
and they would have to head inside.

"What sports do you like to play?" Timmy asked.

"I play ultimate Frisbee with guys from work and
occasional softball game." Reed flexed his mitt. He'd cor
a long way from the gawky, uncoordinated kid he'd on
been. Sports were now fun, not torturous as they'd be
growing up, and he enjoyed working out at the gym.
like to squeeze in a little golf, too."

"Girls play softball."

Biting back a grin, Reed wound up like a major leag
pitcher then threw the ball underhand. "So do grov
men."

"Baseball's better." Timmy caught the ball with t
edge of his mitt, tossed the ball back into the air and caug
it with his bare hand.

"Nice trick."

"My dad taught me that one."

And that's when it hit Reed. Timmy might share a ge
ture, a dimple and coloring with him, but his personal
was more like Art's. The same athletic ability, the sar
confidence, the same showmanship. He envied the relatio
ship Timmy must have had with Art. That's what Re
wanted with his son. And what about Art's relationsh
with Samantha, a voice asked him. Reed ignored it. "I
must have shown you a lot of things."

"I wish he'd taught me how to throw a curve ball befc
he had to go to Heaven."

"You have plenty of time to learn," Reed said. "I dor
know too many eight-year-olds who can throw cur
balls."

"How many eight-year-olds do you know?"

One. "I know you."

Timmy didn't laugh. Instead, he got a faraway look
his eyes, reminding Reed of Samantha when she'd be

nger and a consummate dreamer. "I'd still like to learn
w. Sometimes…"

'What?" Reed asked.

'It's nothing."

From the way Timmy pressed his lips together, Reed
w it was something, but he wasn't about to push. He'd
rned that from Samantha when she'd wanted to know
w Timmy's geography test had gone. Being a parent was
ot more complicated than Reed imagined. Samantha's
p was one thing, but he needed to find a book to tell
n what to say and do. Reed readied his mitt for the next
s. "Okay."

But Timmy held on to the ball. "I haven't told anyone
ut this. Not my mom or even my grandma."

'You don't have to tell me." Reed tried to sound as
nchalant as possible. He flexed his glove again to loosen
the stiff leather. "Unless you want to," he added.

Timmy took a deep breath and exhaled slowly. The con-
sation hung in the air. "Sometimes I have these dreams
d my dad is with me. We play ball or go for a walk or
on the grass and talk." He stared at the baseball in his
d. "It's only a dream, but it seems so real. It's like my
d is with me again. So I sometimes pretend he's still
e."

It wasn't as startling as "I see dead people," but Reed
w gaining Timmy's confidence was a huge step in their
ationship. At the same time, Reed saw how much Timmy
rshipped Art. Reed's nemesis might be dead, but he was
y much alive in Timmy's mind. Reed didn't want to
ew up, but he didn't want to be in competition with a
ost for his son's love, either. "Dreams can be special."

'You don't think it's weird?" Timmy asked.

'Not at all." Reed adjusted his mitt. "It's perfectly nor-
l. I'm sure you miss your…him."

Tossing the ball into his mitt, Timmy nodded.

The sadness in his son's eyes made Reed's chest tight
He wanted to pull Timmy into his arms and tell him
erything would be okay, that he had a father with him.

But Reed couldn't rush things. That wouldn't be fair
Timmy. Or Samantha.

Reed wasn't about to let her down or do something
jeopardize his relationship with Timmy. Besides, R
knew how his son felt. His own father hadn't died, but h
been gone enough it felt as if he wasn't ever coming ba

"When I was little, my dad traveled a lot." Reed
membered the loneliness of being the only male in a hou
ful of females. His mom and sisters had been great,
he'd longed for his father to return, to do male things
gether like playing catch, shooting hoops and watch
sports on TV. But it hadn't happened. Not until Reed
in high school and a total geek. Too old for a lot of
activities he'd wanted to do as a boy. "I dreamed ab
him being home with me, all the time."

Timmy stared at Reed. "Did you miss him?"

"A whole lot," Reed admitted. "All the other kids' d
would show up at school events, but mine was never the
Some days were hard."

Other days had been unbearable. Reed had begun
blame his father for all his problems—his insecurity,
lack of confidence, everything. Including being a geek.
time and maturity had shown Reed he'd been wrong
blame his father. Things weren't perfect between them,
they were better.

"I know," Timmy said. "No one but Cody Dono
and you understand. Well, Cody used to before his
moved back from North Carolina. Now Mr. Donovan
always around."

Once again Reed fought the urge to sweep Timmy up
his arms and make everything better. Not that Reed ha
clue how to do that. Nor would he be around to make s

things were going well for Timmy on a daily basis. Once
Reed was back in Boston, his son would be on his own
again and hurting. Hell even if Timmy lived in Boston,
Reed wouldn't be around much. Like father, like son. No,
he didn't want to go there. "That must be hard on you."

"I'm used to it." Timmy tossed the ball back to him.
"So do you know how to skateboard?"

Confession time was over. The interrogation was back
on. Reed hoped he made the switch as easily as Timmy
had. "No, but I've always wanted to try."

"I, uh, could teach you." Hope gleamed in Timmy's
eyes. "If you want to learn."

The corners of Reed's mouth tugged upward. "I'd like
that, but you'll have to be patient with me. I was a bit of
a geek when I was a kid and I'm still trying to catch up."

Timmy frowned. "Am I going to be a geek, too?"

"Why would you think that?" Reed asked.

"Because my dad isn't here and yours wasn't around
when you were a kid."

Damn. Reed wanted to smack himself. "No, Timmy.
You will never be a geek."

Timmy drew his brows together. "Why not?"

"Because…"

You have me.

But Reed couldn't say the words aloud. "Your mom is
aware of stuff like that. My mom wasn't. You're lucky to
have the mom you do."

Timmy didn't look convinced.

"Trust me. You'll be fine." Reed meant it. He might not
live with Timmy but he would be a part of his life somehow. And that would make Reed part of Samantha's, too.
His chest tightened. "You can always count on me. Even
when I'm in Boston."

"You'd keep me from turning into a geek?"

"Yes."

"Cool." Timmy waved. "Hi, Mom."

Reed turned. Samantha walked toward them, her arms crossed in front of her. "It's getting cold out here, don' you think?"

The temperature continued dropping, but all he could think was how great Samantha looked in her gray sweater and black jeans. Jeans that fit just right, especially in the hips. If he kept staring at her, he wouldn't be cold for long. He forced himself to look away. Samantha wouldn't appreciate him thinking about her like that. Hell, she wouldn' want him thinking about her at all. Better not tell her about his dream last night. If only it had been real....

"Why don't you play for a few more minutes and then come in for some hot cocoa?" she suggested.

"But, Mom, we're having so much fun."

"But, Timmy, if you catch a cold, you won't get to spend any more time with Reed," she countered. "Don' forget he's leaving this weekend."

That was four days away, but it didn't seem long enough. So many questions about how to be involved in Timmy's life needed to be answered. And what about his improving relationship with Samantha? He didn't want distance to send it back to ground zero. If anything, he wanted them to be friends by the time he returned to Boston. He'd better get busy.

Timmy blew out a puff of air. "Okay."

She glanced at Reed, raised five fingers and mouthed the word "minutes." Nodding, he checked his watch. It was up to him. This was the first time Samantha had asked him to do something for her involving Timmy. Was this a test or did she simply want help? Reed didn't know, but Timmy would be inside before the five minutes were up.

As soon as she was back in the house, Timmy removed his mitt. "Do you want to see how I stole second base during the regional play-offs?"

Reed smiled. "I'd love to see that."

Chapter Seven

The front door opened to sounds of laughter and baseball. Samantha dropped the scoop of cookie dough onto the baking sheet and licked what batter remained on the spoon.

If only it were Timmy and one of his Little League teammates coming inside instead of Timmy and Reed. But she couldn't complain too much. Not after she'd overhead Reed telling Timmy he would never be a geek and how lucky her son was to have her for a mother.

Reed's words had been sweet. Samantha hoped he meant them. She didn't want Timmy hurt, but if Reed hadn't been speaking the truth about being there for him, it might be better if her son found out now before he was used to Reed being a part of his life.

Their life.

A jumble of thoughts ran through her head. Part of her anticipated sharing the milestones of Timmy's life with Reed, but the other part dreaded it. That was the part of her wanting to share more than just their son with him. She bit the inside of her cheek.

Footsteps sounded in the entryway.

"Take off your shoes." She placed the pan of cookie in the oven and set the timer. The first batch was sitting on the cooling rack.

Plop, kurplunk, boom-boom. From experience she knew those sounds had been Timmy's mitt, his baseball and hi shoes.

He ran into the kitchen and skidded in his socks to stop. "Do I smell cookies?"

"You always smell cookies, but yes, I'm baking cookies The cocoa's ready." She took a closer look at him. Dir stained his jeans and his fleece pullover. Mud streaked hi hat and hair. His socks left dirty footprints. "You're filthy."

"Aw, Mom." Timmy dusted his hands on his pants "It's just a little dirt."

"A little?" Samantha stared in disbelief. "I was jus outside. Where did all the dirt come from?"

"What dirt?" Reed stepped into the kitchen. He wore hunter-green turtleneck and jeans. He looked less intimi dating, more approachable in the casual clothes. She like it. A lot. Too much. He looked more like the college-boy Reed, the one she'd been head over heels in love with Maybe he could change into a suit.

She moistened her dry lips. "On Timmy."

"Oh, that dirt." Reed smiled, reminding her of when they'd gone wading in a stream near his parents' house and gotten soaked. They'd ended up kissing and getting covered in mud.

Her gaze lingered on his full lips and she remembered how nice it was to kiss not only then, but under the mis tletoe, too. He kissed better now....

What was she thinking? His clothes didn't matter, no did his lips. And forget about his kisses. Samantha focused on their son.

Her son.

"So what happened?" she asked.

"I wanted to show Reed how I stole second base during the regional play-offs," Timmy explained.

"The first time, he didn't get dirty," Reed said. "But I asked him to show me a second time and he slid into a puddle."

Timmy drew his brows together. "It was more like a pond."

"Boys," Samantha muttered. She had two of them right here. "Did you forget about having dinner at your grandparents' tonight? They're back from Roanoke."

She wished Helen and Frank had stayed there the entire week. Samantha didn't think they would guess the truth, but it wasn't worth the risk. They would turn away from her and Timmy, the way her own parents had, if Helen and Frank learned Timmy wasn't their natural grandchild.

Reed might be Timmy's biological father and a part of his son's life now, but no one must know the truth. The realization saddened her. Made her wish she could go back to the past and undo all that had happened over the years. Not just for Reed, but for all of them, including Art.

Looking at the ceiling, Timmy grimaced. "I forgot. I'll go change clothes."

"Not good enough." She pointed to the hallway. "Into the shower, all-star."

"I had a shower last night."

"Too bad."

"But the cookies and hot cocoa and Reed—"

"Now," she ordered.

Mumbling to himself about when he was a grown-up, Timmy shuffled down the hallway.

"Wow," Reed said.

As he stared at her, she tried to ignore how the color of

his eyes resembled chocolate—her absolute favorit
"What? The mean mommy tactics?"

"You weren't mean, you held your ground." He leane
against the kitchen counter, the casual pose making hi
look as if he belonged. "I'm impressed. That's got to b
why Timmy's such a good kid."

Reed's compliment surprised Samantha. Her cheek
warmed. "Th-thanks."

"So what's the secret?" he asked.

She removed a plate from the cupboard. "Secret?"

"To being a good parent and knowing what to do. An
not to do."

This was about Timmy, not her. Or them. And that's th
way it should be. Disappointment squeezed her heart. Sh
stiffened, more aware of Reed and his effect on her tha
she wanted to be.

"There is no secret," she admitted. "I learned a lot b
watching Art's parents interact with Timmy. The rest wa
and still is a lot of trial and error and common sense."

Reed's lips tightened. "Isn't there a book?"

"About a million, but every child is different. Th
chances of finding one book to fit your situation are slin
What works for one child won't always work for another.'

He drew in a sharp breath. "What happens if you mak
a mistake? You could scar a kid for life."

His lighthearted tone contrasted with the serious glint i
his eyes. This was important to him because of Timmy. /
warm glow flowed through her. Reed was nothing mor
than a man desperate to be a good father to her son.

And his son.

Reed seemed to care about Timmy and wanted to do hi
best by him. How could she fault Reed for that? Sh
couldn't, which was part of her growing problem. On
she'd realized last night when he'd asked for her help. Sh
needed to maintain her distance from Reed both physicall

and emotionally, but he was making that harder to do. Samantha rinsed a wooden spoon.

"I would hate to do anything to hurt Timmy," Reed added.

Why did he have to say the right words? It was killing her. "Mistakes made with love seem to only leave a scratch that heals pretty quickly."

"I hope so."

The way he said those three words reminded her of Timmy. "Just give it time."

But he was leaving on Sunday. They didn't have much time. At least this trip. Samantha bit her lip.

Reed started to speak but stopped himself. He ate a piece of cookie dough from the stainless mixing bowl instead.

"What?" she asked.

"You're such a natural with Timmy," Reed said. "It's hard to believe you didn't want to have kids."

"I never said that."

"Yes, you did." He reached for one of the cookies cooling on the stainless rack, and she swatted his hand. Reed grinned. "I was helping you study for your geometry final—"

"Mr. Lester's class." She groaned. "I was sure I would fail."

"You got a B."

"B-minus." Her parents had been furious and yelled at her for messing up her chances to get into Harvard like her brother. She'd said the University of Virginia would be fine by her. Not that she'd ended up there, either. An associate's degree from the local community college was all she'd managed. With a baby, a husband and a job, she'd been thrilled to earn that. "But I never said I didn't want kids."

"You did," Reed said. "I was drilling you on problem-solving techniques. You said learning all of these theorems was a waste of time. You were going to major in public policy and go to law school. Lawyers, you said, didn't need to know geometry."

"Well, it's true." She handed him one of the warm cookies. "But that has nothing to do with having kids."

"Yes, it does." Amusement twinkled in his eyes. "I said you wouldn't be able to help your kids do their math homework if you didn't know geometry, and you said you weren't having kids because you had to make the world a better place for the children already here."

"I did say that, didn't I?" She covered her mouth with her hand. "That's so hard to believe, when I couldn't imagine not being a mom. Timmy is my life. Without him…"

This was all very strange to her. He hadn't cared enough about her to contact her in nearly nine years, but he remembered a random comment she'd made about not having children. "I can't believe you remembered I said that."

"I remember a lot of things, Sam."

Sam.

The way he said her name brought back a rush of memories. Good memories about Reed she shouldn't be remembering. Studying, kissing, making love….

But the way she felt had nothing to do with the past.

Reed took a step toward her, his face mere inches away from hers. "You were so beautiful then. You still are."

The look in his dark eyes made her think he wanted to kiss her. Worse, she wanted him to kiss her.

As he lowered his head to hers, the shrill ringing of the telephone shattered the quiet moment.

"I'll get it," Timmy yelled from the rear of the house.

Reed backed away. A haze of feelings and desires left her holding on to the counter. She couldn't believe what had almost happened. What she'd wanted to happen.

Timmy bounced into the kitchen, reminding her that he could have walked in on them at any time. "That was

Grandma. I told her Reed was here, and she invited him to come over to dinner with us tonight. Isn't that great?''

Great? That wasn't the word Samantha would have used. Suddenly a near-miss kiss didn't seem so bad. It was one thing for Reed to spend time with Timmy away from public view and possible gossip. But for the three of them to have dinner with Helen and Frank…

Her heart hit the floor and kept right on going.

What was she going to do?

Sitting in the Wilsons' living room, Reed leaned back in the leather recliner. His appetite had been fully sated by the delicious roast beef dinner, and he wanted to relax.

All through dinner Samantha had been exchanging concerned glances with him. No doubt his attempt to kiss her had her rattled. Him, too. But it was only due to physical proximity and chemistry. Nothing more. Chances were, they wouldn't get another opportunity like that. Reed ignored the disappointment the realization brought. At least meeting the in-laws was going well.

Until tonight Frank and Helen Wilson had been two strangers. Art's parents. Nothing more. Sure, Samantha and Timmy lived in a cottage on the edge of their property, and Timmy normally spent his afternoons at their house while Samantha worked, but the Wilsons had been all but invisible to Reed. They hadn't been real.

Now they were.

''The Raiders are going to be hard to beat at home.'' Frank Wilson sat on the couch with the sports page spread open across his lap. He was a tall, muscular man, a former professional football player, who towered over his petite wife. Where Art had made Reed feel like a lesser man, Frank didn't.

Timmy sat on the arm of the couch and peered over

Frank's shoulder. "The Jets are going to win. I like their quarterback."

"The Raiders have a good quarterback, too."

Back and forth, the two tried to determine their fantasy football lineup for this week's games. Reed tried to keep up with the conversation, but gave up with so many players and teams and stats being discussed. If he took the time to watch a game, he wanted to enjoy it, not analyze it.

He stared at the blizzard raging outside and thought about the Wilsons. Frank and Helen were down-to-earth and friendly, two of the nicest people Reed had ever met. They made him feel like one of the family. And family was everything to them. Especially Timmy, who was the center of Helen and Frank's world. Everything revolved around their only grandchild, and that explained why they'd been so welcoming to Reed. He'd become important to their grandson so that made Reed important to the Wilsons.

That's where it got sticky. It wasn't a complication, but a consideration. Reed would have to consider Helen and Frank when the truth about Timmy was revealed. And with Frank's heart condition, Reed understood why Samantha wanted to keep the truth a secret and he was willing to wait a little longer. He would never want to hurt anybody with the news. And the more time he spent with Timmy, the more Reed realized there was no reason to rush anything. They all had some adjusting to do.

"Okay," Frank said. "We'll go with the Jets quarterback and the Tampa Bay defense."

"Bet we win the week, Grandpa."

He winked. "Bet we do, too."

As Reed watched the two interact, he felt a stab of envy. Frank's love for Timmy was so strong Reed could almost touch it. This was what being a dad was all about.

He thought about his own father. Until Reed started working, he'd never understood his father's dedication to

s job—the appeal of weeks on the road and only a few
eekends home. But now he did. To get ahead, one had to
e committed. To support a family, one needed a job.

But that didn't make it any easier for Reed now that he
as a father. Especially when Timmy needed a dad who
ould coach Little League or attend a school play or help
a science fair. A dad like Frank. A dad that Reed didn't
now he could be.

"Are the coaches finished picking their Sunday line-
os?" Helen asked as she entered the living room.

Samantha followed her in. "I hope so by now."

Reed's mouth gaped. She wore a white lace-trimmed
oron over her clothes. Domestic and sexy. The combina-
on sent his pulse racing and his temperature soaring.

Chemistry. That's all it was. All it could be.

And that was fine with him.

Physical attraction was something he understood. And
ould handle. Just like he could handle another opportunity
kiss Samantha. Nothing wrong with kissing.

She pursed her lips. "I only wish you put this much
ought into math assignments."

Timmy rolled his eyes. "Mo-om."

"I know, honey." A wry grin graced her full lips. "Fan-
sy football isn't the same. It's less work."

"More fun," Timmy countered.

Reed had to admit the kid had a point. What normal
ght-year-old kid liked doing homework. Well, Reed had,
ut he hadn't been normal.

"Timmy and I selected a great lineup," Frank said.

"Our team is going to win." Confidence laced each of
immy's words.

"Good for you." Helen stood. "We can celebrate your
ocoming victory with dessert."

Timmy rubbed his palms together. "I hope it's some-
ing chocolate."

"Sit down, Helen." Samantha's gaze returned to Reed once more. "I'll get it for you."

As she headed to the kitchen, Helen sighed. "I swe that girl never lets me do anything around here. Not ev my own dishes."

"That's because she loves you," Timmy explained.

"And we love her." Helen wrapped her arm arou Timmy. He leaned against her, soaking up the grandmot erly attention and the love. "You, too."

Reed shifted in his seat. He wondered if Timmy wou love Reed's parents as much as he loved Helen and Frar A bigger question was would Timmy ever consider Re his father. That one had him concerned.

"Do you know what's even better than being a parent' Helen asked.

Not being one? No, that was definitely the wrong answ

The idea of being a parent was slowly sinking in, b Reed hadn't a clue how to respond. Where was Samant when he needed her? "No idea."

"Being a grandparent." Helen kissed the top of Timmy head. "I have the best grandson in the entire world. T smartest, too."

"And a pretty good ball player." Frank tickled Timm

"Just wait until Little League starts and you'll see ho good I've gotten." Timmy pretended to pitch. "I'm goi to learn how to throw a curve ball and make the all-st team."

"Doesn't he remind you of Art?" Helen's voice was fι of pride.

"My dad was the best." Timmy's smile lit up his fac "I want to be just like him."

Reed felt as if his throat had closed shut. And that when it hit him. He would never be a father like Art Frank. No matter how hard Reed tried, it wasn't going

appen. The best he could hope for was to be like his own
ad. Was that going to be enough for Timmy?

The kid had no father. Anything had to better than noth-
g. Right?

"Time for dessert," Samantha announced, carrying
lates with slices of cake on them.

Timmy juggled two plates with extralarge pieces. "It's
evil's food cake."

Helen smiled. "I hope you like chocolate, Reed."

"I do." He took a plate from Timmy. "Chocolate is one
f my favorites."

"My mom loves chocolate," Timmy said.

Reed remembered making s'mores with Samantha. She
ad only wanted the chocolate pieces and had him feed
1em to her one bite at a time. As he had placed the choc-
late on the pink tip of her tongue, she had taken his finger
1to her mouth.... The memory rekindled forgotten feel-
1gs. And some not-so-forgotten ones, too. Reed smiled. "I
1member."

Samantha's startled gaze shot to his. "You do?"

"I told you, I remembered a lot of things." Staring in
er eyes, he vividly recalled what had happened next.
'Like making s'mores during spring break."

She stared at a forkful of cake as if it were the most
1teresting thing in the world. Her cheeks flushed. No doubt
1e was remembering, too. S'mores had led to some more
1ving.

"Samantha has always been a chocoholic," Helen said.

The color of Samantha's cheeks deepened. She shrugged.
'*Most* people like chocolate."

"*Most* people couldn't eat an entire box of chocolate-
overed cherries in one sitting." Frank laughed. "And want
1other box before she went to bed."

Timmy's eyes widened. "A whole box?"

"In case you forgot, Frank, I was pregnant with

Timmy.'' Samantha tilted her chin. ''I couldn't help it if
craved chocolate-covered cherries.''

Her grin told Reed she wasn't upset at the good-nature
teasing. It reminded him of his family's get-togethers ar
all the joking around the dinner table, but he wasn't in tow
often enough to attend most of them.

Timmy stopped eating his cake. ''You still eat a lot
those cherries, Mom. Are you pregnant?''

''No, I'm not.''

''So Grandma's right.'' Timmy giggled. ''You are a ch
coholic.''

Samantha sighed. ''I give up.''

She would never give up without a fight. Reed liked th
about her, respected it, too. The more he learned about he
the more he saw how far she'd come on her own. ''At lea
I know what to get you for Christmas.''

''Don't even think about it.'' She glared at him, but I
heard the amusement in her voice.

''Not unless you get her more than one box,'' Frank sai

''I'd say she deserves at least two boxes.'' Reed laughe
''Maybe three if she's been a good girl.''

''I've been good.'' She winked. ''Almost perfect.''

Desire hit Reed low and hard. His mouth went dry. He'
buy her a case of chocolates if...

''I've been good, too,'' Timmy said. ''What are you go
ing to get me, Reed?''

For a moment he'd forgotten the reason he was her
This wasn't about Samantha and how much he wanted t
kiss her. This was about Timmy. Reed smiled at his so
''Whatever you want, kiddo.''

Chapter Eight

The snow stopped falling long enough for them to make the short walk home. Three hours at Helen and Frank's had been long enough. Samantha had kept waiting for disaster to strike, but it hadn't. Her in-laws seemed to like Reed and didn't think it strange he wanted to spend so much time with their grandson. Of course, in their eyes Timmy was the best thing since the twilight buffet discount at Sara's Family Restaurant, so who wouldn't want to be with him?

Standing in the entryway of her house, Samantha removed her boots. Strains of "Winter Wonderland" came from the living room. Timmy must have forgotten to turn off the snow globe. "We need a new weatherman. Light snow flurries? It's a near whiteout, as if someone pulled a switch and opened the heavens."

Reed clipped Timmy's gloves to his jacket. "Too bad it's not December twenty-fourth so we could have a White Christmas."

"I hope it keeps snowing and snowing—" Timmy removed his hat and handed it to Samantha "—all night long, so I don't have to go to school tomorrow."

A chill came over her as she hung up Timmy's hat. "Any more snow and we would have been spending the night at your grandparents' house."

Timmy grinned. "That would have been fun."

"But crowded," Reed added. "I'd better hit the road before the weather gets any worse."

"No." The thought of Reed on the snow-covered roads sent a trickle of fear down her spine. She'd lost one man who loved her to an accident. She didn't want to lose another. Not that Reed was her man. He wasn't. Or that he loved her. He didn't. But he meant a lot to Timmy. She had to think of her son. "Look at the snow outside. The roads will be terrible."

Reed studied her, his gaze cool and contemplative. "What do you suggest?"

Mixed emotions surged within her. She had to do the right thing. The only thing. "You could stay here."

Timmy brightened at the suggestion. "I can sleep on the top bunk and you can sleep on the bottom one."

Reed's eyes darkened. "Do you think my staying here is a good idea?"

"Yes." Timmy was practically bouncing up and down.

No. But she didn't have any choice. "The roads are too unsafe for you to be out driving on them."

"I didn't know you cared," Reed said.

She didn't, care that was. Maybe a little if she was honest with herself. But it wasn't a lot. Samantha bit her lip.

Timmy stared up at Reed, near worship in his eyes. "I care."

"Thanks, kiddo." His gaze found hers. "What about you?"

His directness made her want to take two steps back. But that would have put her outside in the falling snow. Better here than here. It was as if he saw right through her. She didn't like the feeling.

"I…I wouldn't want anything to happen to you," Samantha admitted.

"Neither would I," Timmy said.

A muscle tensed at Reed's jaw. "If you're sure it isn't a problem."

"No problem."

And the Appalachians were just a few little hills. But no matter how uncomfortable having him sleep under the same roof would be, the alternative—sending Reed out to the icy, snow-covered roads—wasn't an option.

The only other time they'd spent the night under the same roof had been at his parents' house, the night Timmy had been conceived. Air whooshed out of her lungs.

Forget about the past. Forget about Reed. Forget about him almost kissing you this afternoon. This was for Timmy. Not Reed.

"Did you bring your pajamas?" Timmy asked.

"No." Reed hung his jacket. "But I don't usually sleep in pajamas."

That was so not what she needed to hear. Not now, not ever. Samantha wrung her hands. Having Reed here was difficult enough. She didn't want to be imagining what he wore or didn't wear to bed. She'd be tossing and turning all night.

She needed distance from Reed. Not that her small house offered much chance of that.

"Come on, Timmy." She touched Timmy's shoulder. "Let's put clean sheets on the lower bunk and get you ready for bed."

He grinned. "And then we can stay up and—"

"Sorry." She caressed his soft cheek. "We don't know if school will be canceled tomorrow or not."

"But, Mo-om." Timmy gritted his teeth. "Reed is here tonight."

"And as far as we know it's still a school night and past your bedtime."

But Timmy wasn't about to be swayed. He wouldn' budge when she tried to get him to move.

"Timothy…"

He stood his ground.

She was too nervous and keyed up to deal with a mis-behaving child. She didn't have the patience. Samantha counted backward from ten, giving herself time so she wouldn't lose her temper.

"Bedtime, kiddo." The sound of Reed's voice startled her. "If school's canceled, I'll be here and we can spend the entire day together."

Timmy's eyes widened. "Cool."

"So listen to your mom and go to bed." Reed squeezed Timmy's shoulder in a sort of one-arm hug. The gesture tugged on Samantha's heart. "You wouldn't want to be too tired to play tomorrow."

"No." Timmy pulled at Samantha's hand. "Let's go, Mom."

"Be right back," she said to Reed.

As Timmy got ready for bed, she changed the sheets and thought about Reed. Samantha appreciated his help getting Timmy to go to bed. Parenting with no backup and no one to support her was hard. It made for long days and longer nights. But she would do whatever was necessary for her son.

Timmy climbed up to the top bunk. "Don't you think Reed would make a great dad?"

Her heart skipped a beat. Samantha couldn't breathe; she couldn't think. Speaking was impossible.

Timmy waited for her answer with such anticipation in

his eyes. Eyes that resembled Reed's so much. The shape, the lashes, the color, the expression. Her chest tightened.

She hoped Timmy would understand and forgive her when he finally learned the truth about his biological father. "I'm sure Reed would make a good father someday."

"I know so. And not someday, either." Timmy sank into his pillow. "Reed would be the best dad in the whole world. Well, almost as good as my real dad."

Samantha saw how Reed seemed more comfortable around Timmy. He was adjusting to fatherhood. As time went on, it would come more naturally. Especially if he spent more time here with them. With Timmy, she corrected.

"I'm sure Reed would be happy you felt that way about him. Don't forget to say your prayers." She kissed Timmy. "Sleep tight."

With Timmy in bed, Samantha made sure there was toilet paper and laid out fresh towels in the bathroom. Reed would be a good father. She wondered what kind of husband he would be.

No, she didn't.

He was her son's father. He would be nothing else.

Reed sat on the couch and concentrated on the proofs for a new ad campaign. The Utopia software was going to be a hit at the trade shows, but Wintersoft still needed to push their current products.

"Working at this hour?" Samantha asked.

"I grabbed my briefcase from the car while you were tucking Timmy in." Reed hadn't noticed she was back. Good. Every time he'd tried working since he'd arrived in Fernville, his thoughts had kept drifting back to her. It was damn inconvenient. Maybe this meant he was past that. "I also made a fire."

"I, uh, noticed. It's much warmer in here now." Her voice sounded husky. She cleared her throat. "Thanks."

Reed glanced back at the ad proof and tried to ignore her watching him. This was due tomorrow. Morning.

"So what are you working on?" she asked.

"An ad. I wasn't supposed to be on vacation this week and we have a deadline to meet." She'd sounded curious, so he patted the seat next to him. "Do you want to see?"

She took a step toward the kitchen. "The dishes—"

"You did them at Helen's." He grinned at her deer-in-the-headlights expression. "I won't bite. And neither will the ad."

Heat rose in her cheeks, but she didn't move closer.

"Did you remember that I do bite?"

The tension on her face vanished. Samantha laughed. "Yes."

And so did Reed. Forget about working right now. Concentrating was out of the question with Samantha nearby and memories of their lovemaking running through his mind. Reed tucked the manila folder into his briefcase.

"What about your deadline?" she asked.

"I'll do it later. I usually put in a twelve- or fourteen-hour day when I'm home."

"Long day."

"Gets me to make the most of my nights." Smiling, he raised a brow. "Are you going to stand up the entire night?"

With a tilt of her chin, she walked to the couch and sat. Her thigh touched his, and a shock jolted him at the contact point. She scooted away.

Smart move for her. Bad move for him.

"Is Timmy asleep?" Reed asked, trying to take his attention off how good she smelled.

"As soon as his head hit the pillow," she said. "You wore him out."

"Isn't that my job?" he asked.

"You're catching on." Her laughter bubbled over and warmed his heart. "Good job."

The compliment was ten times better than any attaboy he'd gotten at work. After seeing Frank in action, Reed was having serious doubts about fatherhood, but she made him feel better. "Thanks."

"You're welcome."

Silence descended. But it was comfortable, not awkward. The same way it had been when they studied back in high school. No need to fill the air with meaningless chatter. He liked it. A lot.

Reed stared at the silly Santa snow globe on the mantel. The tiny light in the windmill seemed to glow brighter.

The lights in the house flickered. Once. Twice. Blackness blanketed the room. The only light came from the fireplace.

"The electricity is out," she said. "I'll get candles."

"No need." Reed leaned back against the couch. It wasn't that dark. If anything, the setting was a little romantic. And he liked that. With her so close, he was getting in the mood for that kiss he'd missed out on earlier. Maybe then he could stop thinking about her and get his work done. It was worth a shot. "The fire is enough."

"No, it's not." Samantha rose, carried over an oil lamp from the bookcase and placed it on the coffee table. She grabbed matches from the fireplace and lit the lamp. "Just in case we need to go to the bathroom or something."

The "or something" made him curious. Everything about her did. He should be more concerned about that than he was. But the only thing that concerned him right now was her kiss.

Not only was there physical proximity and chemistry, the oil lamp added to the romantic ambiance. He wasn't going to be able to help himself. Or stop himself.

Samantha sat, clasped her hands together and placed

them on her lap. So prim and proper. But he'd experienced the passion lying beneath the facade and wanted to break through.

"Want to play a game of chess?" she asked.

"When did you take up chess?"

"I guess it would be too hard to play without any lights."

"Probably." Reed noticed she hadn't answered the question. He inched closer and rested his arm against the back of the couch. If she hadn't been sitting ramrod straight, it would have been around her. "Isn't this nice?" he asked.

"Uh-huh."

The tone of her voice told him it was anything but nice. Good, he was getting to her. They were even. "Is anything wrong?"

"Just tired."

Wind rattled the window. Samantha shivered. He remembered storms had frightened her before.

Reed squeezed her shoulder. "Storms still get to you?"

"Sometimes."

This had to be one of those times. She was so tense. He remembered how he would rub her shoulders before a big test. That had put her at ease.

"Let's see if I can help you relax." He gently massaged her neck. All her muscles tightened beneath his palm.

"You don't have to do this."

"I want to." Though the more he touched her, the more he wondered if this had been such a good idea. He caught a whiff of her shampoo. Mango. The cold winter's night could quickly turn into a hot summer one. He wouldn't mind. "You take care of everything. Everyone."

"That's what moms do."

"It's time someone took care of you."

Reed wasn't the man for the permanent position, but he

was here now. And looking forward to doing this part of the job.

"Uh-huh." She stiffened. "I mean, no. I don't. Moms are used to taking care of ourselves."

Reed leaned closer and whispered, "You're not just a mom. You're a woman."

She sucked in a breath.

Damn. He sounded like a player and didn't like that. This was Samantha. He shouldn't be putting the moves on her. He needed to stay in control. All he wanted was a kiss. He didn't want to scare her off. "Relax."

"I'm trying."

She sounded exasperated.

"Try harder."

So did he.

"I think you should stop."

Reed jerked his hands away. "Doesn't it feel good?"

"Yes," Samantha admitted, and he touched her again. "But this could lead to…something."

"Something can be good." Reed wound his fingers in her soft, long hair and rubbed her scalp. Man, this was nice. "Isn't this good?"

A sigh escaped her lips. She was going limp. "Yes, but…"

"Do you really want me to stop?"

"Not really."

He knew it. Reed grinned. "I'll keep going."

"Please do," she murmured.

"I'll do whatever you want me to do," he admitted.

A beat passed. "Is that a promise?"

Her question hung in the stillness of the air. Samantha hoped the dark hid the blush staining her cheeks. She couldn't believe she'd thought the words, let alone spoken them out loud. She hadn't flirted in years. But it was coming back to her.

With Reed working magic with his fingers, it was difficult to pretend she wasn't a woman and he wasn't a man.

"You're tensing up again," he said.

She couldn't help it. His nearness was exciting and disturbing. The scent of him surrounded her. Her pulse quickened.

She glanced Reed's way, his profile dark against the light from the oil lamp and fire. "Sorry."

And she was sorry. Sorry for so many things. Both present and past. Most especially the past.

"Apology accepted." He kneaded her back. Slowly, methodically, perfectly. "Now relax. Again."

The humor in his voice made her relax. A little. "Quite the taskmaster, but I remember that from your tutoring sessions."

"If it wasn't for me, you would have never passed algebra."

"Very true." He rubbed away the tightness from her right shoulderblade. Talk about great hands.

"Do you know what my favorite part of tutoring you was?"

His warm breath caressed her neck. Goose bumps covered her skin, yet a rush of heat pulsed through her. The urge to run away was strong, but she couldn't move. Not with Reed's hands unraveling years worth of knots and tension.

"The snacks and sodas?" she suggested.

Laughing, he pressed down on either side of her spine with his thumbs. "I liked how we talked about the future and our dreams."

"Me, too." She remembered all he had wanted to accomplish. Reed's dreams could have been blueprinted and handed to every future business leader in America. But she doubted anyone had the perseverance or the brainpower to accomplish all he'd set out to achieve. "Your dreams have come true."

"Not all," he admitted. "I want to be promoted to a Senior Vice President and one day be CEO of my own company."

Very ambitious. And worrisome. "Have you thought how your job and dreams will be affected now that you know about Timmy? They don't seem too compatible with fatherhood."

"I've thought about it." Reed rubbed her upper arms. "But we don't live in the same town, so I would never be part of Timmy's life 24/7. With all the latest telecommunications technology, I can keep in touch with him wherever I am. We could hook up video conferencing equipment."

She understood Reed's work commitments, but Timmy deserved more than a telecommuting dad. "You can't play catch across an ocean."

"We can play computer games together via the Internet."

Reed seemed to have an answer for everything, and that pleased her. He wasn't taking all of this lightly. "You've put some thought into this."

"A little." He massaged her shoulders again until she felt as if she would melt off the couch. "The most important thing is what's best for Timmy."

Relief washed over her. She smiled. "I'm happy to hear you say that."

"I'm happy you're happy." A trace of laughter was in his voice. "What about your dreams?"

All her dreams had died nearly nine years ago. With him. She stared at the smoke rising from the oil lamp and disappearing into the shadows above. "My dreams are all about Timmy now."

"I don't believe you." Reed stopped rubbing her. "Samantha Brown always had dreams."

She shrugged, but the last thing she felt was indifference. "Samantha Wilson doesn't."

He raised her chin with his fingertips so she had to look into his eyes. A dull ache spread through her at the thought of what might have been. She shrugged away from his hand, but he wouldn't let her go. The way he stared made it hard for her to breathe. Excitement rippled through her.

A warning bell sounded in Samantha's head. Get away from him. Now. But she couldn't, didn't want to, though she knew it was the smart thing to do.

"Sam—"

"Reed—"

"Shhh." The brush of his fingertip against her lips was nearly her undoing. "I may regret this in the morning, but I can't help myself."

As he lowered his mouth to hers, logic had her forming the word no, but the sound never escaped. She hadn't wanted to stop him.

His lips touched hers gently. Almost politely. Miss Manners would definitely approve. He wasn't pushing. If anything he was holding back to see if she was ready for this. Or more.

Part of her was ready. But it was the other part that concerned her. Taking this any further would only complicate matters and lead to more grief and heartache. She'd had enough of those to last a lifetime.

But his kiss felt so good. It wasn't polite anymore.

A mix of chocolate cake and red wine with a hint of hot cocoa and a dose of Reed, his kiss was more satisfying than dessert. And contained less calories, too. She didn't want it to end.

As the kiss continued, the fire slowly reignited within her. Between them. Things were heating up. Fast.

Time to stop.

Easier said than done. Reed had one hand on her lower back and the other in her hair. As he wove his fingers through the strands, she had trouble thinking. Action was impossible.

She'd only kissed two men in her life—Art and Reed. She knew she could stop there. While Art's kisses had been comfortable, Reed's were hot, making her forget everything except how she could keep him kissing her for the rest of the night. His kiss made her feel like a rosebud ready to blossom inside a hothouse. Just a little more…

Forget about stopping.

His warmth chased away the cold in her heart. His strength made her feel secure and safe. His taste left her wanting more.

Samantha wanted this kiss. She wanted to be in Reed's arms. She wanted to pretend, if only for a moment, that her life hadn't turned out the way it had.

Urgency drove her. Longing, too. Parting her lips, Samantha leaned into Reed. He took the hint and pulled her closer. The pressure against her lips increased. Demanding more and more…

The air seemed electrified, vibrant. The scent of the pine of the Christmas tree stronger. The blackness in the room darker. The ticking of the Christmas carol clock louder.

Hunger seemed to overtake him, a driving hunger matching her own. As he pulled her even closer, she arched against him and felt the pounding of his heart against her chest. It matched the rapid beating of hers. She might want this, but so did he. The knowledge sent heat rushing through her.

It was as if she were back in high school, discovering Reed for the very first time. But this was different, better, real. She felt such a sense of belonging in his arms. Something she hadn't felt before.

Reed the boy would have been fumbling with her clothe
trying to undress her. Now she wanted to undress hersel
And him. Not that she would. That's how they'd gotte
into trouble in the first place. But Samantha could imagin
it. She could imagine a lot of things at this moment.

He lifted her onto his lap and showered a path of kisse
from her mouth to her earlobe. She moaned, fueling Reed'
kiss. He found her lips again and not a moment too soor
She wanted this; she wanted it so much.

The kissing continued. The touching and exploring, too
She didn't know how long they sat in each other's arm
lips locked together, but suddenly Reed drew the kiss to a
end. "If we don't stop now…"

Samantha didn't want the feelings to end. She glance
at the fireplace. The fire was dying. A total contrast to th
way she felt inside. She'd never felt so alive, so desirable
Her heart pounded as if it had just awoken from hiberna
tion. Her blood boiled through her veins. Nerve ending
tingled and danced, reminding her what being human wa
all about. "What if I don't want to stop?"

"Remember what happened the last time you said that?"
he asked.

Timmy.

In a flash, light filled the room. The lamp on the en
table blinded her. The interiors of the porcelain Christma
village pieces on the mantel lit up. The Christmas tree twin
kled once again. Even the snow globe was turned on, musi
playing and the windmill sending snow on top of Santa.

Samantha was still sitting on Reed's lap and slid off. Sh
felt a sudden coldness. Yet his easy smile sent tingles rac
ing all over her. Uh-oh. Tingles were not a good thing. Lik
his kisses, they were to be avoided at all costs.

Time for some distance. Samantha scooted away from
him only to hit her hip on the couch's arm. It wasn't fa
enough. The North Pole wouldn't be far enough.

"I'm sorry." Leaning toward her, he tucked a strand of hair behind her ear. "You deserve so much more than I can give you."

But as he said the words, desire filled his eyes, desire for her.

Chemistry. That's what he had called it at the wedding. Something a cold shower or a walk in the snow could extinguish. Samantha moistened her swollen lips. That wasn't enough to make her risk her heart or her family. Nothing was. Especially Reed Connors.

Enough snow had fallen to make it impossible for them to make it into town the next morning. The from-out-of-nowhere snowstorm continued throughout the day.

That night Reed sighed as he lay on the bottom bunk of Timmy's bed. If the snow kept up, he would be here tomorrow, too. Just great. Another day of playing house.

Okay, watching *It's a Wonderful Life* and using a bell off the Christmas tree to give about a hundred angels their wings had been fun. And he had never known there were so many different ways to decorate sugar cookies. Or that Samantha was a real estate tycoon when it came to playing Monopoly.

But Reed was ready for it to end. He had work to do. At least he'd gotten the ad proof in on time. But the rest of his work was piling up. And he had found out this afternoon that he had to be in Frankfurt on Monday morning for a meeting.

He rolled over but couldn't get comfortable. Who was he kidding? Sleep was futile. He wanted to blame it on work. Or rather his lack of time to work. But that wasn't the case. The reason for his insomnia was Samantha.

Each time Reed closed his eyes, images of her filled his mind. Images of her in the kitchen, in his arms, in his bed. Any more of this and he would need another cold shower.

Reed didn't like it. Nor did he get it.

He didn't want a girlfriend. The mother of his son wa
not someone he could have a fling with. Samantha deserve
the picket fence, the dog in the front yard, the cat insid
and a houseful of children. A happily-ever-after marriage
That's why he'd stopped kissing her the other night eve
though he had wanted to continue.

Thinking about his lips pressing against her soft mouth
tasting her sweetness and warmth, feeling her heart bea
against his sent Reed's temperature soaring to record highs

Intoxicating and addictive.

That's what her kisses were, and though confused abou
her, he wasn't the least bit sorry he'd given in to tempta
tion. He'd do it again in a nanosecond if she wanted hin
to. And that made zero sense. But Reed thought he'd foun
a reason this afternoon while he and Timmy were reading

Samantha had to be an enchantress who cast a spell o
him. Nothing else would explain his actions. Or how sh
was the only person who had ever interfered with hi
thoughts. Magic was the only logical explanation.

Only if the sky were purple, a voice mocked.

Reed hated that it was most likely true.

He hadn't felt this way about anyone. Not even Saman
tha when she was younger. He had to make it stop. Now.

A strange noise filled the air. It sounded like a ball bein
tossed in the air and caught in a baseball mitt.

"Timmy?"

No answer.

As Reed crawled out of the lower bunk, the soun
stopped. He checked on Timmy, who was sound asleep
Reed adjusted the comforter over him so his small bare fee
were covered.

What had that noise been?

As he made his way to the kitchen, he glanced at th
closed door leading to Samantha's bedroom. Dead silenc

greeted him. No doubt Samantha had no trouble sleeping and was tucked into her nice, warm bed.

Strike that.

Samantha and the word bed didn't belong in the same sentence. Not in his current state. Reed grimaced and entered the kitchen.

"You're up early," Samantha said, sitting at the kitchen table with a large glass of milk and a plate of cookies in front of her. She wore a pair of gray sweats and an oversize thermal shirt. Her hair was all tousled and she looked sleep rumpled.

Sexy.

Aw, hell.

"I couldn't sleep," he admitted.

"I had trouble myself." She combed her fingers through her hair, and Reed wished he could be the one to do that. "What happened last night was a mistake."

This was the first time they'd been alone since their kissing. He fought the urge to pull her into his arms and show her no kiss between them would ever be a mistake. As he stared into her eyes, he seemed to lose himself in the pools of blue. The feeling was so intense he looked away. No one should be able to affect him like this. Magic spell. It had to be. "You're right."

"So you agree?"

He nodded.

"Thank goodness."

But Reed didn't feel as relieved as she sounded. He was disappointed. But there was no other way. If Timmy weren't here, Reed wouldn't be here. He couldn't forget that.

The corners of her mouth curved up. She pushed the plate toward him. "Would you like a glass of milk and a cookie?"

He took a snickerdoodle. "Thank you."

They ate cookies in near silence. The only sound was the storm outside.

Reed wiped his mouth with a napkin. "I've been meaning to tell you, but I understand why you don't want to tell Helen and Frank about Timmy and me."

Samantha held on to her jelly jar glass. "You do?"

"It's going to be hard news for them to take, so I don't mind waiting."

She took a sip and wiped her mouth. "Thank you. You don't know what this means to me."

Reed knew. He could see it in her eyes and only wished he could do more. But he couldn't. "Timmy's got two sets of grandparents. He can wait a little for the third set."

She stared at her half full glass of milk. "He will never have three sets of grandparents."

"But my parents—"

"My parents disowned me after I got pregnant." As her voice faded, she ran her finger along the rim of the cookie plate. "They said I had always been a disappointment, but this was the final straw. They kicked me out of the house."

The Browns had seemed a bit stuffy. They had pushed Samantha and her older brother, Charles, hard. But Reed couldn't imagine any parent disowning their child. Poor Samantha. Things had fallen apart for her after Reed had left Fernville. He inhaled sharply. "How could your parents do that?"

"I've asked myself that question for years." Her gaze clouded. "I haven't seen them since I graduated high school. They moved to Florida two months later and never told me."

That was after his parents had moved back to Boston. No wonder he hadn't heard what happened. Samantha had needed him back in Fernville. If only he'd known…. Guilt crept down his spine. "What about Timmy?"

''They've never met him.'' Her lips tightened. ''They don't acknowledge his existence. It's…hard.''

''I can imagine.'' But Reed couldn't, not really. If he had known about Timmy years ago, his parents would have stood by him no matter what.

''My family never liked Art. They said the only thing he'd ever be is trouble. But they liked you. When I told them I was pregnant, my mom said if I'd been with you instead of Art this never would have happened.'' She laughed but didn't sound at all amused. ''Pretty ironic, don't you think?''

''I'm sorry, Sam.''

She shrugged, but Reed could tell she cared a lot more than she would ever admit.

''I can't make your parents change their minds, but I can tell you that my parents are going to love Timmy. When they find out about him, they are going to want to make up for lost time and spoil him rotten. He will have another set of grandparents who love him completely. I promise you that.''

''Thank you.'' Her closemouthed smile tugged on Reed's heart. ''That means a lot to me. And will to Timmy, too.''

Samantha looked at him, and for a moment he felt a sense of completeness he'd never felt before. He wished he could promise her so much more than he had.

But that wasn't possible.

Not now or ever.

Chapter Nine

The snow kept falling through the night, but the North Pole weather was finally moving east. By tomorrow, Saturday, they would no longer be housebound. Samantha couldn't wait.

She stirred the bowl of white icing they were using to decorate the gingerbread house. She wanted things to go back to normal and that meant Reed leaving. She needed a break from him.

A long break—like nine more years.

Sure, the three of them were having lots of fun—building a snowman, throwing snowballs at each other and watching her favorite holiday movie *It's a Wonderful Life* and several others. But enough was enough.

Hanging out with Reed was almost cozy. No more kisses, because they'd both agreed their kiss the other night had been a mistake. But all their activities—except when Reed was taking or making a work-related phone call—were family oriented. She couldn't forget the three of them weren't a family. Would never be a family. Reed was here because of Timmy, not her.

So why was a war raging inside her?

A battle against her attraction for Reed. An attraction no
longer based on a fantasy and so much more than the fairy
tale she'd created in her imagination so many years ago.
His compassion, openness and the way he was with Timmy
appealed to her both as a mother and as a woman. Especially as a woman.

But she couldn't forget she was a mother first.

She had to protect Timmy and her family first and fore-
most. Yes, there were sparks between her and Reed. He
was going to be a part of her son's life, but she couldn't
believe in anything more. If not for Timmy, Reed wouldn't
be here. Come Sunday, he would be gone. And she had no
idea when he was coming back.

"Mom." Timmy sat at the kitchen table with Reed putting gumdrops on the roof of the gingerbread house. "We
need more frosting."

She added powdered sugar to the icing and stirred. "It's
almost ready."

She glanced at Reed. He wore a pair of sweats and a
long-sleeved T-shirt Timmy had found in the back of his
closet. Art's clothes. But Reed hadn't complained or said
a word. She respected that. Respected him.

A little more sugar and the icing was the perfect consis-
tency. She filled the decorating bag and carried it to the
table. "Do you want to outline the windows?" she asked
Reed.

"I'll stick to the roof." He puffed out his chest and deepened his voice. "Roofing is a man's job."

"A man's job," repeated Timmy.

"Sorry, but I don't do windows." She handed Reed the
bag of icing. "Besides, the elves are eating more of the
shingles than are making it onto the roof. I need to get
more."

As she returned to the kitchen, Reed raised the tube of

icing in the air. A stream of white fell from the metal t
and he caught it with his left hand. "How does this thir
work?"

"You're smart." She poured gumdrops and peppermi
candies onto a plate. "I'm sure you can figure it out."

"I think he needs help, Mom," Timmy said.

Icing dripped over Reed's hand. What looked like pan
flashed across his face. "Yes, I need your help."

"It's like a tube of toothpaste, only more sensitive
being squeezed," she explained. "Or do manly men co
sider brushing teeth a woman's job, too?"

A sheepish smile stole across his face. "Sorry."

"You're forgiven," she said. "But you still have to ou
line the windows."

With a sigh he went to work on the windows. With h
lips slightly parted, his tongue was flipped over with th
tip showing between his teeth. Just like Timmy did whe
he concentrated.

The resemblance between the two sent her heart han
mering in her chest. She took a deep breath and anothe
Thank goodness Helen and Frank weren't around to notic
it.

Was this how life would be from now on? Wonderin
when the truth was going to be discovered? Afraid her fan
ily would be ripped from her? Her house? Everything? Sa
mantha didn't want to live like this. She couldn't. She an
Reed would have to figure something out. Maybe whe
Timmy visited him in Boston. She had no idea how sh
would afford it or the time since weekends, with wedding
were her biggest days for business. But business wasn't a
important as her son. She would figure a way to do it.

Samantha opened a package of red licorice and placed
on the cutting board. Anything to take her mind off the pa
sitting at the kitchen table, who looked more like father an
son with each passing moment.

"Have you asked her yet?" Timmy tried to whisper, but amantha could still hear him. She focused on slicing the corice into smaller pieces.

Reed placed the bag of icing on the table and wiped his ands with a paper towel. "Not yet."

"You have to ask her," Timmy pleaded.

She couldn't hear Reed's reply. Whatever they were talking about sounded important to Timmy. A guy thing? She dded the licorice to the plate of candy and carried it over the table. "The house looks great."

Timmy bit his lip. "Reed wants to ask you something."

Samantha bit back a grin. "What did *you* want to ask e, Reed?"

As he reached for a peppermint candy, his fingers rushed her hand and tingles raced up her arm. She gripped e plate tighter.

"Would you mind if I took Timmy to the mall tomorrow the weather clears?" Reed asked.

"I want to buy you and Grandma your Christmas presents," Timmy explained. "I've been saving my money. nd I promise I'll be good and stay close to Reed."

"I wouldn't let anything happen to him," Reed added.

"I…I…" Samantha's mind was reeling. What if Reed t the truth slip? What if someone saw them and put two nd two together? The questions made her weak in the nees. She placed the plate on the table and sat. "I know, ut—"

"Please, Mom." Timmy leaned toward her. "We won't e gone long. And I'm going to buy you a Christmas presnt."

"You don't have to buy me a present."

"I want to buy you a present," Timmy countered. You're the best mom in the whole world."

She sighed. "Compliments aren't going to get you anying."

Timmy shrugged. "You're still a good mom."

Reed's gaze never left her, but he didn't say anythin
She appreciated that, but it made her feel guilty. Maybe sl
wasn't being fair to him. He'd been great with Timmy th
week. And Reed was leaving on Sunday. Only two da
away. She ignored the ache inside her.

This would be one of his last times with Timmy. Sl
realized the two needed time alone.

And she needed time away from Reed. His relationsh
was with Timmy, not her. Something she would have
get across to him. Something she would have to rememb
herself.

"Okay," she said finally. "You can go."

Timmy ran over and hugged her. "Thanks, Mom."

Smiling, she held on to him, longer than she normal
did. "Just promise me you'll do two things. Do what Ree
says and buy me a really good present."

Timmy grinned. "I promise."

On Saturday the mall was crowded with shoppers. Peop
carried bags filled with presents for friends, family ar
loved ones. A chorus of high school students sang Chris
mas carols. Stores were decorated in their holiday finest–
wreaths, trees, ribbons and lights.

Reed's assistant usually did his shopping for him. Sl
enjoyed hitting the stores and making his busy life easie
He had never felt like he was missing out on anything b
avoiding the December shopping rush, until now. Ree
found himself humming along with the cheerful musi
wanting to buy things on a whim and looking for jolly ol
St. Nicholas.

"Do you know what you want to get your mom?" h
asked.

Timmy nodded. "It's at the girls' store."

Reed followed Timmy to a boutique full of every typ

f collectible imaginable—figurines, teapots, spoons, dolls, tuffed animals. A floral fragrance scented the air. The overwhelming use of pinks and purples made Reed feel out of place. Definitely a girl's store. One Samantha must love.

Timmy walked to a display of lighted porcelain Christmas villages similar to the houses on Samantha's fireplace mantel.

"I want to buy her this one." He pointed out a woman street vendor selling flowers from a basket. A flower cart went with the figurine. "I earned the money doing stuff for my grandparents."

"Your mom will love it," Reed said.

A smile erupted on Timmy's face. "She likes this one the most, but it costs too much money."

He pointed out a house—an elaborately designed gable-roofed cottage, actually—that was charming and elegant at the same time. Reed did a double take. The piece's resemblance to his family's former house in Fernville stunned him.

Timmy touched one of the gables. "Nice, huh?"

Emotion clogged Reed's throat. He could barely breathe, let alone speak. Why would Samantha want that house when it was identical to the place where Timmy had been conceived? So many memories would be associated with t. Memories she had put behind her and forgotten. Reed didn't get it. Unless…

She wanted to remember. Unless she wasn't as immune to the past—their past—as she pretended to be. Unless she cared.

She still had to care.

"May I help you?" A well-dressed woman with ink-black hair asked. Her name tag read Margery.

"I'd like to buy the flower lady and cart," Timmy said, sounding more like he was twenty-something than almost eight.

"I'll get a boxed set from the back room." Marger
smiled. "Anything else?"

Reed stared at the cottage. He shouldn't… Oh, what th
hell. "And one of those gabled houses, too."

Timmy's eyes widened. "You collect houses?"

Reed imagined the hand-painted cottage displayed in hi
leather and glass furnished apartment and tried not to laugh
"It's for your mom. A Christmas present."

"She's really going to like it," Timmy said. "And you."

Smart kid. That was the entire point. But where woul
the liking lead? Additional kisses, or more? Too bad ther
wasn't enough room in Reed's life for more.

"You must really like my mom or you wouldn't b
hanging around so much."

"I like your mom, but I like you, too," Reed sai
"That's why I've been hanging around. If you'd prefer
wasn't here—"

"No," Timmy interrupted. "I mean, I still have to teac
you to skateboard. Maybe not this time, but the next…"

"Definitely."

Timmy smiled.

With their packages gift-wrapped, they continued shop
ping. Timmy bought a scarf for Helen and a book to hol
baseball cards for Frank. Reed purchased warm pretzels an
lemonade for their lunch. A stop at the candy store provide
dessert, as well as a box of Samantha's favorite candy.

She'd been on Reed's mind. He couldn't stop thinkin
about their kiss. It had felt so right, so perfect. She had t
feel the same way. He'd seen the desire in her eyes, fe
her surrender in his arms. But it went deeper than that
Spending the past two days and nights with Samantha an
Timmy had made Reed care more about them. But th
growing and deepening of his emotions made him uncom
fortable. He hadn't felt this way in years and wanted it t
stop. Now.

Feelings made him vulnerable. He couldn't be vulnerable in business and he sure as hell didn't want to be that way in life. It was easier to keep his distance. Safer, too.

Reed saw a sign for the North Pole and Santa Claus. A giant red arrow showed the way. "Have you seen Santa yet?

Timmy nodded. "I had my picture taken with him for my mom."

Reed wanted a picture. He could keep an image of Timmy close when he was back in Boston. Tomorrow. Now to figure out how his son would fit into his life once he was gone. E-mail, telephone calls, video conferencing. Lots of people telecommuted with their jobs. He could be a telecommuter dad. Maybe that would work with Samantha. No, that would be a long-distance relationship. He wasn't looking for one of those. "Would you mind visiting Santa again so I can have a picture?"

"Sure." Timmy looked up at him. "But I want to stand this time."

"Not a problem."

Timmy beamed. "I knew you would understand that us guys don't have to sit on Santa's lap."

Reed's confidence soared. Maybe he was getting the hang of fathering.

On the way to see Santa, Timmy pointed to a sports memorabilia store full of autographed balls and photographs and jerseys. "My dad liked that store."

With the display of baseball stuff up front and a Santa wearing a Yankees uniform, Reed could see why Art would have liked it. A strange time to be pushing an off-season sport, but Reed knew software marketing, not retail.

The Yankee Santa seemed to be pointing his mitt at the jewelry store next door. High end for a regional mall in the middle of nowhere Virginia. Necklaces, earrings, bracelets and rings filled the glass cabinets.

In a window a large diamond, set in platinum with smaller stones on either side, was displayed prominently against black velvet and caught his attention. Hell, the ring was practically calling to him.

He stopped walking. "Wait a minute, Timmy."

Shimmering, sparkling, elegant. The ring would look so perfect on Samantha's finger.

Where had that come from? It was an engagement ring. Not a friendship ring. Not a promise ring. An engagement ring. Engagement equaled marriage unless you were a reality TV show contestant.

Marriage seemed a bit…sudden, extreme, out of the question. It was the last thing Reed wanted, needed. But she was having kids, and now he had a son.

He glanced down at Timmy. Not there. Reed did a three-sixty. No sign of Timmy.

He was gone.

Reed's stomach plummeted. Every one of his senses went on alert. "Timmy."

He scanned the crowd and ran to the sports memorabilia store. Timmy had to be here. Somewhere. Reed searched the other nearby stores, but couldn't find him.

Timmy must have wandered off. Boys did that. Unless someone had taken him. Reed's panic rose.

If anything happened to Timmy…

"Timmy." No answer. People stared at him, but Reed kept calling for him. "Timmy."

No answer.

Reed's blood pressure skyrocketed. Adrenaline surged. He had to do something, but he didn't know what.

He saw a uniformed security guard and rushed over to him. "My s-so—the boy I was with is missing. His name is Timmy Wilson. He's eight years old, brown hair about so high." Reed raised his hand about four and a half feet

The guard pulled out a walkie-talkie and alerted the other guards. "Has Timmy ever wandered off before?"

"I don't know." Reed continued scanning the mall. "I'm a friend of the family from out of town."

"What's he wearing?"

Reed tried to remember. "Jeans. A blue sweatshirt. No that was yesterday. He's wearing a green sweatshirt. With a black T-shirt underneath. I think."

Reed was a total failure at being a father. He couldn't remember what Timmy was wearing. A part of him wanted to die. The other part, the larger part, just wanted to find his son.

"Does Timmy have brown hair and a blue fleece jacket?" the guard asked.

Reed remembered the jacket Samantha had washed after Timmy's sliding-into-second-base exhibition. "Y-yes."

"He's waiting in line to see Santa." The guard put away his radio and pointed. "He's waving at you."

Overwhelming relief washed over Reed at the sight of Timmy waving. "That's him." Reed forced the words from his mouth. "Thanks."

As he walked toward Timmy, Reed's legs felt weak. His pulse was still racing. He'd never felt anything like the happiness of knowing Timmy was safe, but at the same time Reed felt as if he'd dodged a bullet.

His anger rose. Not at Timmy, but at himself for letting his son out of his sight. It had only been for a couple seconds, but that had been too long. This was a part of being a parent Reed had never imagined. One he never wanted to experience again. Too bad Timmy was too old for those harness or wrist straps little kids wore.

Reed had to face the truth. He wasn't cut out for being a father.

"Why didn't you tell me where you were going?" He wrapped his arm around Timmy and had to force himself not to squeeze too tight. "I thought something had happened to you."

"The line was getting long so I wanted to make sure I got us a spot." He pointed to all the kids and parents behind him. "Good idea, huh?"

This wasn't easy. Reed brushed his hand through his hair. Anything to keep from pulling Timmy into his arms and never letting go until he was old enough to go to college. At the same time Reed wondered if he could catch a flight to Boston tonight instead of tomorrow morning. He wanted out of here now. He wasn't getting the hang of parenting. He'd been deluding himself. And Timmy could have paid the price.

"You can't wander off. You have to tell me or your mom or another adult where you are going." Reed tried to keep his voice low and steady. "Do you understand?"

Timmy nodded. "Sorry."

"You're safe." Reed forced a smile. "That's the most important thing."

Timmy looked up at him with a hopeful gleam in his eyes. "Were you worried?"

"Yes," Reed admitted. "I was really worried."

"I'm worried about you," Helen said.

"Why?" It was past closing time, and Samantha was in the workroom putting supplies away after making centerpieces for a dinner party at the mayor's house. She stared at her mother-in-law who had dropped by the flower shop a few minutes before.

"You seemed upset when you were at our house for dinner," Helen said. "Is something wrong?"

Samantha didn't know where to start. Art, Timmy, Reed. She shrugged instead. "A lot has been going on."

"With Reed?"

Maybe if Samantha ignored the question, it would go

away. "I have some leftover flowers, would you like to take them home."

"The answer is yes, but don't try and change the subject."

Darn, so much for it going away. She pulled out a sheet of clear cellophane and placed it on the worktable. "Reed's nice," she said. "Timmy likes him."

Helen studied her intently. "What about you?"

Samantha didn't know where to begin. She picked up two white lilies and three red roses. "I like him."

Helen smiled. "I think it's wonderful you and Reed found each other after so many years apart. And the timing couldn't be better."

The only other person who knew about her and Reed was Art. Samantha held the flowers in midair. Water dripped from the stems, but she didn't care. Water she could clean up. Losing her family would be a lot messier. "What do you mean?"

"Timmy needs his father."

No. Helen couldn't know.

Samantha dropped the flowers onto the floor. Every one of her muscles tensed. Her stomach flipped three somersaults before knotting itself inside out. She knew what was coming.

This was her worst nightmare. One she'd lived through with her own parents. She hadn't ever wanted to experience it again. That's why she'd tried so hard all these years to be a perfect daughter-in-law, to not make any mistakes...

"I'm not blind, Samantha," Helen admitted. "I see the resemblance between Timmy and Reed."

Air rushed from Samantha's lungs. Her heart pounded. She struggled to salvage the situation. Timmy would be devastated. She would be, too. "Just because they have the same color hair and eyes and a dimple—"

"It's more than that, sweetheart." Helen picked up the

flowers and placed them on the plastic wrap. "When we were playing Pictionary the other night, both Timmy and Reed had the same expressions on their faces. You know the stubborn determination that shows up around the jaw line. They didn't just resemble each other. They looked exactly the same."

Samantha's world tilted on its axis and came tumbling off. It was all over. All over. She clutched the counter to keep from falling to her knees. "I...I...I'm so sorry."

Her voice was barely a whisper. Her lower lip quivered. Tears stung her eyes. She'd lost the only family Timmy had. Would ever had.

"Don't cry." Helen hugged her, but Samantha couldn't relax into her mother-in-law's comforting embrace. "It's going to be okay."

"No, it's not. I l-lied." She'd messed up again. Helen and Frank wouldn't love her anymore. They wouldn't love Timmy. She stepped out of Helen's embrace for the last time. No more hugs, no more love, no more family. "I didn't tell you the truth and now you hate me."

"I don't hate you, Samantha." Helen lifted Samantha's chin with her fingertip. "Family goes deeper than blood and DNA. We will always love you and Timmy. Art didn't leave us only a grandson, he left us a daughter. Nothing will ever change that. Frank feels the same way."

Samantha's chest tightened. "Frank knows?"

Helen nodded.

"But his heart—"

"Can handle it."

Samantha waited for the catch. What she would have to do to remain a part of their lives and in their hearts. Whatever it was, she would do it.

"As long as you're a part of our lives, we can handle anything."

"I don't understand," Samantha said. "I was sure you'd be upset, angry, never want to see us again."

Helen's eyes shone with compassion and tenderness, not hatred and revulsion. "I'll be honest, we were surprised. Shocked, actually. Then I remembered something Art told us after the two of you got married. He said some people thought he *had* to marry you, but he wasn't marrying you because of the baby. He was marrying you because he loved you and couldn't imagine living the rest of his life without you." Helen's eyes glistened. "Art told us the baby was more like a wedding gift from an old friend. I didn't think much of it then, but now I understand."

"Thank you." Samantha forced the words out when all she wanted to do was cry happy tears. Art *had* loved her with no strings attached. His parents, too. It was possible. Maybe Reed... Hope filled Samantha's heart. "Thank you for becoming my parents, for taking care of Timmy and me and giving us so much."

"Thank *you*, honey." Helen squeezed her hand. "I don't know how we would have survived these past three years without you and Timmy. No one can ever take Art's place, but having you and Timmy around made it easier."

"I don't know what we would have done without you and Frank."

"Then we're even," Helen said. "But we're pleased to see you are finally moving on with your life. With Reed."

"I don't know if I would call it moving on." Samantha added a few stems of greenery to the flowers, wrapped up the bouquet and tied a silver ribbon around them. "I'm not sure what we're doing."

"I see how Reed looks at you. It reminds me of the way Art looked at you." Helen wiped tears from her eyes. "Art loved you and Timmy more than anything, but he wouldn't want you to spend the rest of your life alone. He would want you to find love again. To find someone who could take care of you the way he did."

Helen made it sound so simple. They had shown Samantha it could be, but still... "What about you and Frank?"

"Frank and I will be wherever you want us to be. Here or say, in Boston. You have to do what will make you and Timmy happiest." She picked up the bouquet of flowers and sniffed them. "We both think Reed makes you happy."

"So do I," Samantha admitted aloud.

Maybe she was making love too complicated. Her entire adult life, she'd been afraid of losing the love of those closest to her. She hadn't been in any position to open herself to new love. But she couldn't continue living like that. She was good enough to be loved for who she was. It was time she started living that way.

And she was going to start with Reed.

Timmy finally reached the front of the line, and he didn't care that it had taken a long time. He felt so good inside, like when he got a good grade or struck a batter out.

Reed wanted his picture and had been worried about him. He must like him a whole lot. That was good because Timmy liked Reed, too.

"You're back," Santa said. "Is this a social visit or do you want your picture taken?"

"A picture," Timmy said. "But not on your lap this time."

"It's not for your mom?"

He was impressed Santa remembered and motioned to Reed, who stood by a computer screen to see how the picture turned out. "No, him."

Mrs. Claus said "smile" and snapped a picture.

"That's Reed. He's nice," Timmy said. "He can't throw a curve ball, but he plays catch. And he likes to play games and knows a lot about computers and helps me with my homework and taught me how to play chess.'' Timmy lowered his voice. ''I want him to be my new dad.''

With a twinkle in his eyes, Santa stared at Reed. ''He would be a good dad for you.''

Yes. Timmy pumped his fist. ''I knew it.''

Santa smiled. ''There's still a lot of work to do if we want to make this happen by Christmas, but I found the perfect helper who's already on the job.''

''An elf or an angel?''

''You'll figure it out soon enough.'' Santa handed him a candy cane. ''Don't forget, you have a job yourself. Do you remember what you have to do to get what you want?''

Timmy nodded. ''I have to believe.''

And he would. With all his heart.

Chapter Ten

It was time to return to Boston. If this afternoon's mishap at the mall hadn't shown Reed that, dinner at the Fernville Pizza Parlor had.

No matter how hard he tried, he didn't belong here.

Families with crying, screaming, laughing children of all ages crammed into the wooden booths and tables. The volume of racket battled with the child-friendly music playing from overhead speakers. The scent of garlic and basil filled the air, reminding Reed this was a pizza joint, not a single guy's version of Hell. At least there wasn't a giant rat—or was it mouse?—character walking around and visiting each of the tables like at his niece's third birthday party.

Reed sipped his root beer. Not as refreshing as a bottle of beer, but the soda was Timmy's favorite.

Timmy stood. "Can I please have money for the video machines, Mom?"

Samantha reached into her purse and handed him a few dollar bills. "Don't go anywhere but the game room."

"I promise I won't." Timmy glanced Reed's way, smiled and ran off to the game room.

At least the kid remembered the promise he'd made at the mall after the disappearance nightmare. Reed hadn't decided whether to tell Samantha about it. No harm, no foul.

The corners of Samantha's mouth curled. "At least tonight he's giving you time to finish your dinner."

Reed wiped his mouth with a napkin and picked up a slice of pepperoni and mushroom pizza. "And for that I'm grateful."

"I'm grateful for a night out so I don't have to cook. I hope you don't mind this place. It's Timmy's favorite."

Reed still couldn't believe Samantha had suggested going out for dinner. Not when she'd wanted to stay home all week. At first, he thought she didn't want him out in public with Timmy, but she had allowed them to go to the mall today. That had been a mistake, but going out tonight had been the right thing to do.

Samantha's home cooked meals and the lively dinner conversations were getting a little too cozy and comfortable. No matter how she might kiss or make him feel, his life was in Boston, not here.

"I eat a lot of pizza when I'm home." Reed forced himself to use that word, to remind himself that home was the apartment where he kept his stuff while working or traveling and not the quaint cottage she lived in. "Or anywhere else."

"I can't believe you're flying to Germany tomorrow," she said. "I've never even been to Canada."

"It's not that far away if you wanted to go."

She shrugged. "I have to take Timmy to Disney World before I go anywhere else."

The temptation to suggest he take them on the trip was strong, but Reed ignored it. His last night in town wasn't the right time for an offer like that. Especially since he had no idea how he was going to be involved in Timmy's life once he left. Phone calls, e-mails, video conferencing? His son deserved better, but that's all Reed could do.

If that, a voice whispered to him. Promises were easier to make than keep. But he didn't want to listen. Not when he knew it might be true.

Samantha reached across the table and touched the top of his hand. A shiver ran up his arm at the point of contact, reminding him how good things were between them. And could be, if he let it happen.

But he couldn't.

Reed thought about Wintersoft. About the upcoming Utopia software release. About what he had to do to become a Senior Vice President. No way he could squeeze Samantha into his life. Timmy was going to be hard enough. Reed pulled his hand from hers and picked up his glass.

Her eyes sparkled like diamonds. She looked so happy and animated. A total change from how she was only a week ago. "So I have some news."

He wished he could capture the expression on her face and take it with him the way he was taking Timmy's photograph with Santa back with him. "Must be good news."

"Very good news." Samantha lowered her voice. "Helen stopped by the flower shop this afternoon. She and Frank guessed the truth about you and Timmy. They're okay with it. Isn't that great?"

"Great," he said, forcing the word from his dry mouth.

But it wasn't great. Not at all. Reed sure as hell wasn't ready to announce being a father to anyone. Not even his son. Timmy was the best kid in the world and deserved the best dad. That wasn't Reed. He'd been thinking about this all day, longer than that if he were honest with himself. Everything about who he was and his life told him that he wasn't father material.

"Nothing is stopping us from telling Timmy or your parents, or the world for that matter."

But there was an obstacle still in the way. Reed drank the rest of his root beer.

Samantha continued. "You'll have to use that brilliant mind of yours to come up with a way to tell Timmy the truth."

"Okay." But he was only saying the words. It wasn't okay. Not even close. He set his glass down. "But we should wait."

"You think?"

Reed forced himself to only nod once. "I'm leaving in the morning. Timmy's birthday is coming up. Christmas, too. And he just met me. We wouldn't want to overwhelm the kid. Too much, too fast."

And I need more time to deal with this.

Her tender expression was one normally reserved for Timmy, and a lump formed in Reed's throat.

"That's so sweet of you to consider the effect on Timmy."

But it wasn't sweet. Reed felt like a jerk. He had only been thinking of himself. Not his son.

He really was the worst father in the world. And soon everyone would figure that out.

It was almost time for goodbye.

Samantha stood at the fireplace, wound the Santa snow globe and turned on the switch for the windmill. As "Winter Wonderland" played, she plopped onto the couch and waited for Reed to finish tucking Timmy into bed.

Her conversation with Helen this afternoon had given Samantha the courage to go after what she wanted. To not be afraid of being loved or having that love taken away because she wasn't good enough or made a mistake or a million other things.

She didn't want Reed to leave Fernville, but she knew he couldn't stay. That left only one option…

Her heart beat faster and she wrung her hands. Breathe, just breathe.

Reed entered the living room, looking more handsome in his brown V-neck sweater with a white T-shirt underneath and jeans than he had when he walked into Timmy's bedroom. His charm reached across the living room and surrounded her like the snow around Santa in the snow globe. Unlike old Santa, Samantha was warm. Perspiration wet the back of her neck.

One corner of Reed's mouth lifted into a slight smile. "I didn't think I was going to get out of there until I showed him my plane ticket back to Fernville."

This gave her the opening she needed, but she was having difficulty breathing. She struggled to fill her lungs with air. She was so nervous. "Timmy's going to miss you."

"I haven't known him that long."

"With kids, it doesn't take long."

Reed was quiet. He was standing near the chair on the other side of the room. Too far away from where she sat.

"Why don't you sit down for a minute?" she asked.

"I have to pack tonight," he said. "I've got an early flight in the morning."

Samantha brushed aside the twinge of disappointment. She knew he had other responsibilities and commitments with his job. "This won't take long."

He sat in the chair across from her. "Shoot."

"I've been thinking about this whole situation and trying to figure out what's the best solution."

"I thought we were just going to wait and see what happens."

"Yes, but…"

She didn't want to wait. A few kisses, shared glances, time spent together as a family and she was ready to believe in one true love and a happily ever after. She rubbed her palms together. She didn't want to scare Reed away by asking for too much, too soon. But she would burst if she didn't do this now.

Samantha continued. "Timmy's so attached to you. He can't wait to see you again, and once he finds out the truth, he's going to want to see you even more."

"That's going to be hard to arrange. I travel most of the time," Reed said. "I'm never home."

"I know…" Her voice cracked. He seemed so distant, making this harder for her. But she had to do it. For once, she had to take the chance. Just like the last time, she had everything to gain, and everything to lose if she didn't take the risk. She wouldn't make the same mistake again. Samantha cleared her dry throat. "It will be difficult for you to be a part of Timmy's life with all your work responsibilities and us living in Fernville."

Relief flashed in Reed's eyes. "You understand."

It wasn't a question. This was going to work. She pushed all her uncertainties away.

"Of course, I do. That's why Timmy and I are going to move to Boston."

Reed's mouth fell open. A second later he pressed his lips together. She waited for him to say something, anything. He didn't. He didn't even smile.

Samantha wrapped her arms around her stomach that was tied up in more knots than all the ribbon on the presents under the tree. "I thought you'd be happy."

"I'm speechless." Reed leaned forward in the chair and rested his elbows on his thighs. "What about the flower shop? And Helen and Frank?"

"I can sell the shop to Ginny. Helen and Frank will either come with us or visit a lot."

"I'm not in Boston much. My job requires—"

"A lot of travel. I know." She didn't understand Reed's

apprehension. It was as if he didn't want them near him.
She spoke faster, as if she could convince him by the sheer
pace of her arguments. Why wasn't he happy? "I've been
thinking of going back to college part-time to get my degree. There are lots of colleges and universities in Boston.
If I got a job at a flower shop and with Timmy and all his
activities, I'd be so busy I wouldn't miss you *that* much."

"My apartment isn't that big."

"I'm not suggesting we get married or move in with
you." She kept her tone light-hearted. He had to be nervous, like her. That's why he was acting so strange. "But
if we're in Boston it'll be easier for you to see Timmy. And
me."

"Samantha."

Reed's serious tone sent a chill down her. "What's
wrong?"

"Moving to Boston isn't a good idea."

She forced a quick smile. He was joking. He had to be.
But he didn't smile back. His words sank in. Weighed
down on her. Made her want to crawl into a hole and cry.
But she wasn't going to let her old fears stop her. They had
stopped her for too long already. She tilted her chin. "Why
not?"

"Your life is here, in Fernville."

"My life is with Timmy," she said. "And his father
lives in Boston."

"Timmy's mother lives in Fernville," Reed repeated.

He didn't get it. She steeled herself to spell it out for
him.

"This isn't only about Timmy." She wasn't about to
settle for whatever love was thrown her way because she
wasn't good enough for anything else or had to earn it. She
was going to get the love she wanted. Helen and Frank had
shown her it was possible. And Samantha wanted it from
Reed. The way he kissed her made her believe he felt the

same way. "It's about you and me. We..." Her voice faltered.

Reed stared at her wide-eyed as if she were speaking a foreign language or had three eyes and an antenna sticking out of her head. "I care about you, Sam."

Okay, this wasn't so bad. Some of her unease dissipated. She moistened her lips. "Caring is a good start."

"That's all I have to give," Reed admitted. "I'm not looking for a family, Sam. I like my life the way it is."

She tried to digest what he was saying, but her heart refused to believe. His words didn't match his actions. The same way they hadn't all those years ago. No, she wasn't going to bring up the past. He wasn't the same boy. He was a man. "I thought there was something between us. When we talked and kissed...I felt—"

"Chemistry," he said. "That's all."

Her heart beat so loudly she couldn't hear anything else. "There's more to it than that. There's got to be more."

"I'm sorry."

He was serious. She'd read it all wrong. The looks, the kisses, everything. She sank back against the sofa, trying to somehow soften the blow to her heart. She'd taken a chance at love and failed. A humiliating, deflated feeling threatened to overwhelm her. She tried to keep the tears from rolling down her cheeks.

Reed didn't want her.

"Are you okay?" he asked.

Samantha couldn't answer. She wasn't okay. He hadn't wanted a family. He didn't want her.

His rejection was like a bullet to her heart, a million times worse than the first time he'd walked out of her life. She wasn't coming to him with a girl's hopes. She had come to him with a woman's heart. There was no misunderstanding keeping them apart, no childish games. She'd been open and honest. She'd offered to leave the one place she felt safe and secure and move to where he was. She'd risked it all. Forget about love with strings attached. He didn't want her love period.

Her heart had been ripped out and a black void stuck in its place. If only that were the case… But it hurt too badly for her heart to be gone.

Reed stood. "I have to go."

She wanted to yell at him. She wanted to scream at him. She wanted to shake some sense into him. But there was Timmy to consider.

There was always Timmy.

Whatever else Reed denied her, she had his son. And she had her son's feelings to protect and fight for. She forced herself to stop shaking.

Samantha knew where she stood in Reed's life, and Timmy had to be her focus.

She picked up the small white envelope from the coffee table, met him halfway across the living room and handed it to him. "Timmy's birthday is on Friday and he wrote you out an invitation himself. He'd love it if you could come."

Reed took the invitation but didn't open it. He shoved it into his jacket pocket instead. Not a good sign, she thought. But she waited for his answer.

What was the matter with him? What was the matter?

Tension stretched between them. The uncomfortable silence seemed to push them farther apart even though they were standing right in front of each other.

Something was wrong, and it had nothing to do with Reed and her. Every motherly instinct she'd ever known had gone on alert. She might have fallen in love with Reed, but so had Timmy. She didn't want her son's heart to be broken the way hers was.

"Aren't you going to open it?" she asked.

Reed's gaze met hers. "I'm not cut out for this."

"Cut out for what?"

"Being a father."

"I don't understand," she admitted. "You are a father. Timmy's father."

"I'd make a lousy father." Reed brushed his hand through his hair. "Don't worry, I won't walk away from my responsibilities. You will have all you need financially. If Timmy needs anything I'm just a phone call or e-mail away."

"Timmy needs you to be a real part of his life." She fought to control her frustration. "Not your money, not your phone calls or e-mails. Only you."

"He deserves to have the best father in the world." Reed sounded so resigned. "That isn't me."

"You're just making excuses."

His mouth twisted. "Today at the mall, I lost Timmy. I looked away for a minute and he was gone."

"What do you mean he was gone? As in disappeared?" Reed nodded stiffly.

"What happened?" she asked, panic rising in her voice. "How long was he gone? Who found him?"

Hurt gleamed in Reed's eyes. "He was only gone a few minutes. He'd wandered off to get in line for Santa, but I didn't see him. A security guard helped me find him."

She took a deep breath. "Okay. It's okay. He was safe. That's all that matters." Her gaze sought Reed's. "I'm sorry I just panicked, but losing a child is a mother's worst nightmare."

"A father's too." The anguish in Reed's voice clawed at her heart. "Don't you see, anything could have happened to him and it would have been my fault. He's better off without me."

"But you found him," she said calmly. She touched his arm, but he shrugged away. "Everything turned out okay."

"This time. What about the next time?"

She understood how he felt. She'd been there herself.
"Do you think Timmy would be better off without me?"

"Never."

"No one knows this. Not even Art." She didn't want to
tell Reed, but she had no choice. "When Timmy was a
baby, I was sitting with him on the couch and the telephone
rang. They say never to leave a baby unattended, but he
was sound asleep. And I knew he couldn't move even if
he were awake.

"But I was wrong. He could move and rolled off onto
the hardwood floors. He was crying so much I wanted to
die. It was my fault and I knew I was the worst mother in
the entire world. But I couldn't just say this is too hard or
hurts too much and decide not to be his mother. It's not a
choice you make."

"Your parents did."

She flinched as if he'd slapped her. She struggled to
breathe, to speak, to make him see the difference between
him and her parents. Between Timmy and her.

"Only because I was never a part of their hearts." She
wanted him to understand. So much depended on it. "If I
had been, the way Timmy is a part of my heart, they could
never have made that choice. Just like I don't think you
can make that choice, either."

This wasn't only about Timmy. This was about her, too.
She couldn't beg. She would be accepted for who she was
or not at all. She had to find the strength to stay strong.
For Timmy.

Reed didn't say anything. He stared at the fireplace.

"Fathers aren't made overnight. It's okay to make mis-
takes." She was battling for her son's father. He needed
Reed. And he needed his son. "You are what's best for
Timmy."

Reed walked to the door and put on his coat.

She forced herself to follow him when all she wanted to

do was crumple to the ground. "What do I tell Timmy about his birthday?"

"I don't know," Reed mumbled.

With that he was gone. Out of her life. Out of their son's life. Samantha slumped against the door and slid to the floor. Tears stung her eyes, and she tried to keep them at bay.

No I'll see you soon.

No I'll call you.

No goodbye.

And like the first time he'd walked out of her life, she got the sinking feeling Reed Connors wasn't coming back. After all these years of believing Reed hadn't loved her, it had come true. He didn't love her. He didn't want her. And there wasn't a damn thing she could do about it.

Friday morning Reed sat at the table in the war room, also known as the executive conference room, with the other Wintersoft executives. The only one not in attendance was Brett Hamilton, Senior Vice President of the Overseas Division, who was on his honeymoon in Scotland with his bride, Sunny.

Lucky guy. Not for getting married, but for being smart enough to be out of the office today. Lloyd Winters's emergency meeting about the Utopia project had already been going for two hours. At this rate, they'd be here all day. Possibly night. Utopia, the newest enterprise financial software, would put Wintersoft way ahead of their competitors. Unfortunately, there was a problem.

"It's not a setback," Nate Leeman, Senior Vice President of Technology, explained. "It's not even that big a deal."

Next to where he'd been doodling Samantha's name, Reed scribbled the words "delayed release" on his notepad. Techies never wanted to admit anything was wrong with their software, but since working at Wintersoft, not one project had been released on time. Just the nature of the beast.

"So how will this affect our projected release date?" Reed asked. "From a marketing standpoint—"

"There is no delay." Nate Leeman's jaw clenched. "The product will ship on time."

"Let's hope so," Matt Burke from accounting said. "Our second-quarter earnings are counting on it."

"Your earnings will be fine."

Matt grinned. "Last time I checked the books they were Wintersoft's earnings, and that makes them yours, too, Nate."

Nate's eyes darkened. "*Our* earnings will be fine. Just like the software. The release date will not change."

Never one to show emotion, Jack Devon, in charge of business strategy, stared at Nate's attempt to diminish the issues facing Utopia with his typical poker face. Grant Lawson's tired eyes widened—the new twins must not be letting the company's General Counsel get much sleep. Emily Winters, however, was alert and not the least bit amused.

Reed retraced the letters of Samantha's name. He wouldn't want to be sitting at Nate's computer today. Poor guy.

"Nate." Emily gave him an encouraging smile. "I understand your confidence in your team, but we have to be absolutely sure. We've committed to the announcement at several trade shows, we've got events scheduled, advertising locked in and the sales collateral prepared," she explained. "If this bug affects the beta test schedule, it will affect the release date. And that affects us."

"I will have us back on schedule by the beginning of the year. There will be no delay to the release date."

"That's only a week and a half away," Matt Burke reminded. "With Christmas vacation—"

"Forget about the holidays." Nate's nostrils flared. "I said it would be done and it will."

"And a bah-humbug to you, too," Chad Evers murmured, the kind of comment Reed would have expected from the Senior VP of Public Relations.

But Reed knew Nate would work late every night and sleep on his office couch if that's what it took. Not that the guy didn't sleep there, anyway. Workaholics R Us. But that's what it took to succeed in this business.

Business.

That had been the last thing on Reed's mind all week. He'd just gotten back from three days in Frankfurt—a world away from Fernville. But that's where his thoughts had been. On Samantha. Night and day. Even during this meeting. He tried to shut off the thoughts and feelings, but couldn't. It *had* to be jet lag.

He was back where he belonged. In control. Well, almost.

No reason to think about anything except the here and now. He had to stay focused on what was important. Wintersoft.

"It's time for a break." Lloyd Winters rose. "Say fifteen minutes, then we'll reconvene and figure out how we can support Nate and his team while they remedy this... situation."

Grant was the first one to stand. He glanced at Emily. "I'm going to call Arianna and see how Christopher is feeling."

Emily smiled softly. "Tell her to give both babies a kiss for me."

With a nod, Grant left.

"I can't imagine what Grant and Arianna have been going through with Christopher," Chad said. "He's so little."

"Only six weeks old," Matt added.

"What happened?" Reed had only stopped in Boston long enough to repack his suitcase and fly to Frankfurt. He had no idea what he'd missed while out of the office for nearly two weeks.

"Christopher, one of Arianna's twins, was sick," Emily explained. "He had a 103 degree temperature and ended up being admitted to the children's hospital for two days. They released him on Tuesday."

Chad sighed. "If it had been one of my kids..."

If it had been Timmy...

Reed got a familiar gut-clenching feeling in the pit of his stomach. The same way he'd felt at the mall. One day, he realized, it could be Timmy. An illness, an injury, an accident. And whether Reed was the best father in the world or the worst, if something happened to his son, it would hurt. Hell, it would kill him.

It's not a choice.

He finally understood what Samantha had meant.

"You look pale." Emily touched his forearm. "Are you okay?"

Reed nodded, but the last thing he felt was okay. He sat at the table and shuffled through his notes. Anything to take his mind off a realization that would change everything. But the words on the page blurred. Reed couldn't see anything except Timmy.

And Samantha.

Damn. Reed might have chosen his life in Boston, but his heart chose Samantha and Timmy. Whether he was in Boston or Fernville, Reed's feelings weren't going to change. Whether here or there, he was going to think about them. Whether he was with them or not he was going to worry about them.

And Reed wanted them with him. He wanted to be with

them, to love them, to protect them. Not for one day or a week but forever.

All this time he thought he was being focused on his career and being successful, but he hadn't. That had been only an excuse. He'd been trying to keep his heart safe by controlling his emotions, his feelings. All his efforts had failed.

And he'd failed the two people who mattered most.

Today was Friday. Timmy's birthday. Reed stood. What the hell was he doing here?

Reed glanced at his watch. If he left now he could make it to the party. Or at least part of it. He had to try. Even if it weren't Timmy's birthday, Reed would go back for Samantha.

As Lloyd reviewed a document, Reed made his way to him. "I need to leave."

"We're not finished," Lloyd said. "I'm counting on your input."

Reed hesitated. Another promotion would make him a Senior Vice President. How he handled the Utopia project could determine it. Hell, this meeting could determine it. But he couldn't disappoint Timmy. Somehow Reed would learn how to be a better father. And he especially didn't want to disappoint Samantha. That's all he seemed capable of doing. It had to stop.

She had put herself on the line. No test this time, only honesty. But Reed hadn't listened. He'd only been thinking of how this affected him. Again. He might have changed from the geeky boy he'd once been, but it hadn't been enough. He was making the same mistake. Only this time he couldn't blame her or Art or anyone except himself. It was all Reed's fault. He didn't deserve Samantha, but that wasn't stopping him. Not this time.

Reed hadn't thought he wanted a family, but that's what

he needed. A family. A wife and a son. And he was going to get it. "One of my people will cover for me."

Lloyd's eyes widened. "This must be important. Work related?"

"It's...personal."

Lloyd chuckled. "When did you get a personal life?"

"About eight years ago," Reed said. "But I only realized it."

"I'm not sure what that means, but go." Lloyd smiled. "Will you be back for the holiday party?"

The political answer would be yes. "I don't know," Reed admitted. "But I'll try."

And if he made it back to Boston in time for the company's annual holiday get-together, Reed only hoped he wasn't alone.

Chapter Eleven

Only forty-five minutes until the end of Timmy's birthday party, and Reed wasn't here. Samantha stuck the first of eight candles on the birthday cake, her heart aching.

The nine boys were coming off the rink, careening into walls and each other, shoving, shouting, having fun. Timmy wore a big grin. Samantha sighed. He still believed Reed was going to show up for his birthday party.

She knew better. For a week there had been no sign of Reed. No calls. No e-mails. No birthday card in the mail.

She watched the boys settle at the table, fighting for position on the narrow benches.

Please don't let your son down, Reed. Don't break his heart the way you broke mine.

Samantha stuck the last candle in and grabbed the matches. Lighting the seventh candle, she sensed a presence behind her. The wide smile on Timmy's face told her who it was before he shouted, "Reed!"

He'd made it. Thank goodness.

But the moment was bittersweet. Frustrating. Painful. He'd come for Timmy. Not her. Reed didn't want her.

Samantha didn't glance back. She was afraid if she did she would cry. But tears didn't belong at her son's birthday party. This was his day, and she wanted to make it special.

She focused on the tasks at hand. It wasn't easy. Her hand trembled as she lit the final candle. Her legs wobbled as she carried the cake to the table. Her voice wavered as she led nine boys in a boisterous rendition of "Happy Birthday."

No matter, she would survive. No, Samantha corrected, she would do better. She would thrive. No more being afraid to make a mistake or take a chance or believing love only came with strings attached. She would live life fully. And someday love that way, too.

Someday. More like some year. About ten of them. Until Timmy went away to college and she would no longer be required to see Reed Connors again.

Timmy leaned over the cake.

"Don't forget to make a wish," she said.

"Already made one." With a twinkle in his eyes, Timmy blew out the candles and looked at Reed. "Now it will come true."

The boys around the table clapped and cheered and asked for big slices of cake with lots of ice cream.

Helen took the cake off the table. "I'll slice it. Frank can dish up the ice cream."

"What am I supposed to do?" Samantha asked.

Helen motioned behind her. Reed. Great.

Samantha might as well get it over with. With a sigh, she turned. Reed stood with a large gift in his hands. He wore a suit and tie as if he'd come straight from work. Mr. Brooks Brothers comes a-calling. Even though she knew he wasn't there to see her, she felt the butterfly sensation in her stomach and the surge of her pulse rate. If only love was something she could turn off with a switch.

But she had to figure out a way to do it if only for a few

ours. Long enough to get through Timmy's birthday. She squared her shoulders and took a deep breath.

"Where should I put this?" he asked.

Ignoring the vise grip on her heart, Samantha pointed to the stack of presents on a nearby table. "Over there."

His smile sent a rush of heat running through her veins. It wasn't fair he had this effect on her. Not after Saturday night when he'd rejected her. Not when she wanted to hate him. She did. But she couldn't.

"Thank you for coming." Samantha forced the words out, keeping her voice cool and steady. She only wished her insides weren't shaking. "It means a lot to Timmy."

"What about you?" Reed asked.

His question squeezed her already hurting heart. Her blood pressure seemed to increase by the second. "Not here," she croaked out the words.

"But I need to talk to you—"

"No," she said through tight lips.

He took a step toward her. "I was wrong—"

"Please," she whispered. "This is Timmy's birthday. I don't want to ruin his special day. And that's what would happen."

Reed's eyes darkened. "Later…?"

A nod was all she could manage. Much later. Perhaps never. All she could think about was Saturday night. *I'm not looking for a family, Sam. I like my life the way it is.*

She wanted him; he didn't want her. But at least he wanted their son. Otherwise he would never have shown up here today. He must have had a change of heart about fatherhood. That's what he'd meant about being wrong. Good for him and Timmy. She could force herself to be satisfied with that. Learn to live with that. But it didn't mean she wanted to talk about it.

With a steadying breath she turned back to the giggling boys. "Who wants more soda?"

* * *

All Reed wanted was to be alone with Samantha. B
now that he had driven Timmy home from the birthd:
festivities, she wasn't there. They'd beaten her to the hous

"This is the best birthday gift." Timmy sat in the midd
of the living room and spun one of the wheels on his ne
skateboard. "Thank you so much."

Smiling, Reed put more presents under the tree. At lea
he had bought his son the perfect birthday gift. Maybe I
should give Samantha her present early. "I'm happy y
like it."

"I love it." Timmy grinned. "This has been the be
birthday ever. A party, dinner out, a movie. Very cool."

"It's been a busy day," Reed said.

Too busy. He needed to talk with Samantha, expla
things, apologize. He understood today was his son's birt
day and Reed was thrilled to be a part of it, but each pas
ing minute made it harder to enjoy himself. He was stan
ing on the edge of something amazing, and he wanted
jump in with both feet. But he couldn't do that witho
Samantha.

He needed her to listen to him. And understand. She ha
to understand.

Timmy looked up at him. "I only wish…"

The longing in his son's voice touched Reed's sou
Whatever it was, he wanted to give it to his son. "Wh
do you wish?"

"I asked Santa for a lot of things this Christmas, inclu
ing a skateboard," Timmy said. "But there's one thing
want most of all."

"What's that?"

"A dad."

Reed's breath caught in his throat. It was too much
hope for. Wasn't it?

"My real dad's in heaven, but I need a dad here wi

ie.'' Timmy picked up a figurine from the nativity scene
itting under the Christmas tree. ''Do you know who this
;?''

''Joseph,'' Reed answered.

Timmy nodded. ''Joseph wasn't Jesus's real father, but
e treated him like a son. Could you…do you think you
ould do that with me?''

His son's request was everything Reed had ever wanted
nd more. His heart overflowed with love for Timmy. He
ouldn't imagine Timmy not being a part of his life. Of his
aily life—24/7.

''I could definitely do that. Come here.'' Timmy did, and
Reed hugged him. ''There's nothing I want more than to
e your dad, but we'll have to see what your mom says
irst.''

Timmy's smile was brighter than all the lights on the
Christmas tree. ''Santa told me all you have to do is believe
nd anything can happen.''

Reed stared at the Santa in the snow globe on the mantel.
He hoped her cool reception to him today wasn't an omen
if things to come. Reed sighed. ''Let's hope Santa is
ight.''

If the snow kept up, Santa was going to need Rudolf to
ead the way on Christmas Eve. Samantha saw the lights
;lowing inside her house. Reed and Timmy were home.
gnoring the dread building inside her, she unloaded the
ags of presents from her car. The rest of the stuff could
vait until tomorrow. The boys had eaten all the cake and
ce cream at the party.

She waded through the newly fallen snow to the front
loor and took a breath. Several actually, to prepare her to
ace Reed. The only bright spot in any of this was Timmy.
His presence would limit the topics of discussion. She

planned to let him stay up as late as he wanted since it wa his birthday.

Feeling chilled to the bone, Samantha stepped insid placed the bags on the floor and removed her jacket. Than goodness for forced-air heating. Warmth crept back into he body.

She walked into the living room. Two steps across th hardwood floor and she froze.

A fire crackled in the fireplace, warming the room wit its flames. The lights on the tree twinkled, bringing th magic of the Christmas season to life. Reed sat on th couch. His sock-covered feet on top of the coffee table.

Her breath stilled.

No man had a right to look so charming, so good. No after working all morning in Boston, flying to Fernville i the afternoon, attending a birthday party with nine ran bunctious eight year olds, eating a fast-food dinner an watching a G-rated kid flick at the cinema.

She pushed aside the rush of attraction, but it wasn easy. With a skateboard on his lap and another next to him he looked as if he belonged. Not only tonight, but ever night.

The scene was so warm, so homey, so right. And tha made her realize how very wrong it was. The flickerin flames provided a romantic glow and cast shadows acros the room, shadows matching the ones in Samantha's hear Reed had made her realize how alone she'd felt for the pa: three years. How alone she would continue to feel. He chest tightened.

"Where's Timmy?" she asked.

"In bed."

She glanced at the clock. "It's only a little past his bed time. On his birthday. And you're here."

Reed shrugged. "He was tired."

"That would be a first." Her voice sounded flat. To match her heart.

The tension and awkwardness in the room were unbearable. She wondered if this was how divorced parents felt when they had to see each other dropping off or picking up kids.

"Timmy got a lot of presents," Reed said.

She stared at one of the skateboards. "Did you have to buy him two skateboards? One would have been enough."

"One of them is for me."

She drew her brows together. "Why would you want a skateboard?"

"Timmy promised to teach me how to skateboard," Reed said. "I thought it would be easier if we each had a skateboard."

"Oh." Samantha realized Reed was going to be a part of Timmy's life. She wished she felt more relieved. But all she could think about was seeing Reed for the next ten years. Even longer with holidays and college graduation and when Timmy got married and had children of his own. Her broken heart shattered into more pieces. "That was nice of you."

"Thanks," Reed said. "Why don't you sit?"

She hesitated. Sitting meant talking.

But even knowing how he felt—or didn't feel—about her, didn't stop his charm from reaching across the living room and drawing her in. Samantha took a step toward the couch but stopped herself. She sat on the chair instead. Anything to maintain some distance.

Reed placed the skateboards on the coffee table and sat straight. "We need to talk."

No, they didn't.

She crossed her legs and uncrossed them. For some reason she was having trouble getting comfortable.

"I'm sorry." His gaze held a look of regret. "I wish I

could say I didn't know what I was saying on Saturda
night, but it wouldn't be true. I knew. It just took me a fer
days to figure out I was wrong. It's okay to make mistake
and I can be a father to our son. I want to be there fc
Timmy and not through e-mails and telephone calls an
occasional visits. But *with* him. As much as possible.''

Samantha was happy for her son, but at the same tim
she felt as if she was on the verge of crying for herself.

"You were right. Loving isn't a choice.'' Reed rose an
walked to the fireplace. "I thought I could shut off m
feelings, but I couldn't. Not when it came to Timmy. O
you.''

Or me?

Her heart seemed to stop beating for a moment. She re
leased the breath she hadn't realized she had been holding

"I realized something about myself today. These pas
eight, almost nine years, have all been about protecting my
self. Protecting my heart.'' He turned on the Santa snov
globe. "Before you, I was the typical nerd—data in, dat
out. But you touched my heart, made me feel things I'
never felt before, and it was scary putting myself out there
I'd never had to risk anything before and when I did it hur
I didn't want that to happen again. I went back to colleg
after spring break telling myself I sucked at relationship
so I should go back to what I was good at—schoolwork.'

Reed had shown her a glimmer of hope, and she wa
clinging to it. But her grip was loosening. She wondered i
she had misunderstood what Reed had meant by ''or you.'
She sank back against the chair, deflated once more. ''I'r
so sorry.'' She forced the words from her dry throat.

"It's not your fault. Not all of it.'' The corners of hi
mouth lifted. "I'm the one who got good at coming u
with excuses. It didn't matter if I was in college or busines
school or at my job. The excuses justified my actions. An
the more I did it, the more turning off my feelings becam

like second nature. It was much simpler not to care, to keep my distance and not get hurt. The worst part was, it worked. Until I saw you again.''

Samantha's gaze flew to his. She clutched the chair.

"You were the reason I shut down my emotions, but you were also the one who opened them back up. Without you, I would still think I was living the perfect life and had everything I could ever want.'' He stared into her eyes and sent her pulse quickening. "But I wasn't, Sam. And I didn't have what I really needed.''

"What's that?'' she asked.

"You.''

Her heart pounded in her throat. She struggled for a breath.

"The perfect life involves feelings, insecurities and love. I have to embrace those things, not try to avoid them.'' He took a step toward her. "Thank you for teaching me that.''

Samantha felt as if she would burst with happiness. It was all she could do to remain seated.

"Life involves risk. Risking your heart. That's what you did on Saturday night. But I wasn't listening. I couldn't.'' As he walked toward her, his voice softened. "Can you forgive me?''

"Yes,'' she said. It wasn't over for them. It was only beginning. "You were the first person who ever loved me for me. No strings attached, no anything. When you went back to college after spring break I wanted to die. I thought what we shared hadn't been real, and that love without conditions was a pipe dream.''

Reed knelt, took her hand and kissed it. Heat emanated from the point of contact between his lips and her skin.

She swallowed. Hard.

"Until you came back into my life, I was living a lie,'' she admitted to him. "Not only about Timmy, but about myself. I believed I had to earn love and work to keep it.

That's why I was so afraid of Helen and Frank finding out the truth about Timmy. They were the only family I had, and I couldn't lose them the way I'd lost my own parents. But I didn't give the Wilsons enough credit. Or myself.''

Samantha leaned toward Reed. She wanted to be closer to him. Much closer. ''By doing that I wasn't really living or loving for that matter I was too scared to do anything but react.''

He squeezed her hand. ''You weren't scared last Saturday night.''

''Yes, I was.'' The same way she was right now. But she wasn't about to stop. ''It was worth the risk. *You* were worth the risk. Are.''

''Come with me.'' Reed laced his fingers with hers, led her to the Christmas tree and sat. ''Tonight Timmy told me what he wanted Santa to bring him for Christmas.''

''What's that?'' she asked.

''A new dad.''

She blew out a puff of air. Reed was here, but she didn't know what that meant long-term for herself or their son. She had high hopes, but the reality was a mystery. ''That's a tall order even for Kris Kringle.''

''I'd hate for Timmy to be disappointed on Christmas morning.'' Mischief glimmered in his eyes. ''I'd love Santa to bring me a son, but there's something else I want.''

''What's that?''

He let go of her hand, pulled a small box from between the branches and handed it to her. ''Open this first.''

She untied the red satin ribbon and opened the box. A black velvet ring box was inside. Her heart slammed against her chest.

''Open it,'' he urged.

Her fingers trembled as she opened the lid. A diamond with baguettes on either side set in platinum sparkled against the black velvet. ''Reed—''

"I want a son, but I want Santa to bring me a wife, too," Reed said. "I want to be Timmy's father, but I also want to be your husband. I thought I loved you when we were younger. But I didn't realize what real love was until I'd come back to Fernville. You were so different—a woman, a business owner, a mother—nothing like the girl I'd put on a pedestal so many years ago. I couldn't help falling in love with you. All over again."

Reed cupped her face with his hand. "This love is different, much stronger than what I felt before. I know less about being a husband than I do about being a father, but I want to be the best I can be at both. The only thing that matters to me is you and Timmy are part of my life. Forever. That's my choice. The only one I can make."

Joy filled her heart. "Oh, Reed."

He took the ring out of the box and held it up. "Samantha Wilson, will you marry me?"

The depth of emotion she felt overwhelmed her. She breathed in deeply and exhaled slowly. Anything to keep the happy tears from spilling out her eyes. "When I found out I was pregnant, I dreamed you would show up on my doorstep, propose and take me away to some magical place. And when that didn't happen, I lost sight of my dreams. Life was still good, but it wasn't the same. That wasn't good for me or for Timmy. Thank you for bringing dreams back into my life. And love."

"Is that a yes?"

"Yes." She laughed. "Yes, I'll marry you."

"And move to Boston?"

Samantha saw the anticipation in Reed's eyes, the hope. She nodded. "Helen and Frank will have to move, too. Or visit a lot."

Reed grinned. "Whatever it takes to make you and Timmy happy."

"That's you." She stared at the ring on her finger. "So, what do we tell Timmy?"

"About getting married?"

"About that, and you and him." Samantha's smile softened. "Timmy needs to know the truth. If not now, someday."

Reed stared at the Nativity scene sitting next to them. "I know a way we can explain it so Timmy will understand. But let's not rush it. We have plenty of time."

"Plenty of time," she echoed.

"Today is just the first of many."

She winked. "Don't you mean tonight?"

"Yes, tonight." Reed lowered his mouth to hers, claiming what was finally his.

Timmy was dreaming about his dad again. He liked dreaming about his dad more than looking at pictures and watching the videos. In the dreams he got to be with his dad, and tonight they were playing baseball on the greenest diamond Timmy had ever seen. The grass smelled like it had just been mowed. His dad was trying to teach him how to throw a curve ball.

Timmy threw a pitch. It didn't curve the way the last one had. He sighed. "I can't do it."

"You'll figure it out. Try again." Art threw the baseball back to him. "You've got a big-league arm, son."

"Just like you."

Art grinned. "Just like me."

Timmy pitched the ball. It was halfway to home plate and started breaking to the right when a strange noise sounded. His dad dropped his mitt, and the ball seemed to disappear. "Time for me to go, Timmy."

"But you'll be back, right?"

"Not this time." Art walked to the pitcher's mound and picked him up. He hugged Timmy until he couldn't breathe anymore. It was the best hug Timmy had ever had in his life and he didn't want it to end. "Things are changing, son. It's time for you to move on. You can't do that with me hanging around."

"But I want you around." The dream started getting all fuzzy, and Timmy got scared. The grass was disappearing. "Daddy?"

"I love you, son. And I'm proud of you." Art smiled. "Remember, I will always love you and your mom. Nothing will ever change that."

"I love you, Daddy."

"Your Christmas present is under the tree."

"But it isn't Christmas yet." Timmy didn't understand. "Santa hasn't come yet."

"Enjoy it." Art waved. "Don't forget, I love you."

"Daddy?"

But the dream was over. His dad was gone. Again.

Opening his eyes, Timmy felt strange. Sad. Worse than when his team lost or he got in trouble for doing something wrong. Maybe it was because the dream was over and he didn't want it to end. Not ever. He scooted to the edge of his bunk bed. One of mom's chocolate chip cookies would cheer him up. Maybe Reed would want one, too. If he was still here…

Timmy climbed down the ladder. He shuffled his way to the kitchen, but noticed the Christmas tree lights on in the living room. Funny, but his mom always remembered to turn them off. She was scared the house would burn down. Maybe that meant Reed was here. Timmy heard "Winter Wonderland" playing from the Santa snow globe.

He took a step into the living room and stopped. His mom and Reed sat on the floor in front of the tree kissing.

The kissing was pretty gross. He was never going to kiss a girl. Not ever. But seeing his mom and Reed so close together gave Timmy a good feeling in his chest. Maybe with grown-ups kissing wasn't so bad.

He started to look away, but saw something glimmer on his mom's finger. He squinted for a better look. A diamond ring. Yes. He pumped his fist and made a silent cheer. He was getting a dad, and it wasn't Christmas yet. Santa had gotten the help he needed. Timmy grinned.

He tiptoed back to his bedroom and stood at his window. It was dark outside. The snow had stopped falling. He continued to stare and wait.

Things *were* changing. For all of them.

A bell rang. Timmy wasn't sure where it was coming from, but that didn't matter. He remembered the line from his mom's favorite Christmas movie.

Smiling, Timmy looked up to Heaven through the one clear patch in the otherwise black sky. "Thank you for helping Santa, Daddy. I hope you enjoy your wings. And I think I can throw a curve ball now."

Epilogue

Emily Winters watched the Wintersoft holiday party in full swing at the New England Aquarium. Smiling snowmen greeted the guests as they entered the main exhibit hall. Food stations were set up on the three floors surrounding the four-story Giant Ocean Tank full of tropical fish, moray eels and giant sea turtles. On the first floor, a band played and several of Emily's co-workers and significant others danced.

Once again, her father, Lloyd, had spared no expense for his employees. And it had paid off. She saw lots of smiles and people having a good time.

As she sipped a glass of spiced cider, she watched a penguin swim through the water. Bet no one told it whom to marry.

"Happy holidays, Emily." Jack Devon raised his glass of eggnog to her. "Quite a party."

"It is." She glanced around. "Nate's the only one missing. The rest of his team made it. Don't tell me he's still working."

Jack nodded. "Someone tampered with the files detailing Utopia. He's trying to determine who."

"Espionage?"

"Could be." Jack took a drink. "Someone has also been accessing the personnel files on several of the VPs in the company."

Emily's stomach clenched. Her father's assistant, Carmella, had legally accessed the top execs' personnel files, but neither she nor Emily had anything to do with the prototype files. This wasn't good. She downed the rest of her cider. "Maybe someone's just curious."

"Curiosity killed the cat," Jack said. "More likely a mole or a spy. Why else would someone poke around where they don't belong?"

She tightened her grip on her glass. "Personnel files don't contain top-secret information."

"No," Jack said. "They contain private information."

"And these two are Emily Winters and Jack Devon. Both Senior Vice Presidents." Reed Connors led a beautiful woman with long, blond hair toward them. They made a striking couple. "Emily, Jack. This is my fiancée, Samantha Wilson."

"Nice to meet you," Samantha said.

As Emily admired her beautiful engagement ring and offered her best wishes, Carmella joined them. She hugged Reed and Samantha. "Congratulations. I'm so happy for you."

"Thanks." Reed grinned. "And thank you for convincing me to attend the wedding in Fernville. Without you, Carmella…"

"Our lives wouldn't be quite so wonderful," Samantha finished for him.

"That's what friends are for." Carmella smiled warmly. "Looks like the entire office has been bit by the marriage bug. Did you know Matt and Sarah have been looking at houses in Newton?''

Reed put his arm around Samantha. ''We'll have to talk to them. We want to find a town on the train line with good schools.''

''So many happy couples.'' Carmella winked at Emily. ''I wonder who's next.''

Emily saw the interest gleaming in Jack's gray eyes. Darn. He'd noticed the wink. Heat rose in her cheeks. He was on to them. Not a good thing. Especially with two bachelors still to go.

''I don't know.'' Reed pulled Samantha closer and laughed. ''But all you singletons had better be careful. I really think there's something in the water.''

* * * * *

Turn the page for a sneak preview of the next
MARRYING THE BOSS'S DAUGHTER
title
featuring Nate and Kat's battle-of-the-sexes
romance:

RULES OF ENGAGEMENT
by Carla Cassidy
on sale January 2004 (RS1702)

Chapter One

Nate Leeman stood at his office window and watched as big, fat snowflakes drifted lazily down from an overcast sky. It always surprised him when somebody mentioned how beautiful Boston could be in January.

As far as Nate was concerned, snow meant only one thing…longer commutes to and from the office. Many a wintry night he had camped out at work rather than fight traffic and inclement conditions. Of course most nights he'd just as soon be here than at home.

Here was his office at Wintersoft Inc. As Senior Vice President of Technology, he commanded a large office outfitted with a wet bar he'd never used, an ornate armoire containing a television, stereo and DVD player he'd never touched and a sofa sleeper he'd never unfolded.

All he cared about sat on his enormous desk…his state of the art computer and supporting equipment. The computer and its programs and files weren't just his work, it was his life, and despite all the security precautions, somebody had violated it.

Now, his computer wasn't alone on his big desk. A second monitor and keyboard set next to his and the sight of it only served to heighten the irritation that had been with him since the moment he'd awakened that morning.

A knock sounded on his office door. "Come in," he called and turned away from the window.

Emily Winters, Senior Vice President of Global Sales and the boss's daughter, entered and immediately sat on the burgundy sofa opposite Nate's desk. "The forecast is for two to four inches by midnight."

"What time does her plane arrive?" he asked. "Her" was Kathryn Sanderson, a private investigator specializing in tech crimes and a part of his past he'd just as soon never encounter again.

Emily looked at her watch. "In an hour."

"Then there shouldn't be any problems," he replied. He hoped his personal feelings about the subject didn't color his words or tone. As far as he was concerned, he wouldn't care if bad weather kept Kathryn's plane circling Logan International Airport for days.

He didn't want her here. He didn't need her help. Unfortunately, he wasn't the boss, Emily's father, Lloyd, was and it had been his and Emily's idea to hire outside help. It had been sheer serendipity that they had chosen a woman…the only woman with whom he'd shared a tumultuous history.

"I've booked her a room at The Brisbain so she'll be close to the office." Emily tucked a strand of her shoulder length brown hair behind an ear, her blue eyes troubled as she gazed at him.

"We've got to get to the bottom of this, Nate. We've got too much time and too much money tied up in the Utopia program for it to be tampered with and leaked to our competitors."

"Trust me, I'm as upset about this as you are," he replied.

She stood and smoothed the skirt of the sapphire dress that perfectly matched the hue of her eyes. "Dad and I are confident that you and Kathryn will be able to get to the source of the security breech. You're two of the best in the business." She headed for the door. "I'll send her in as soon as she arrives so you can put your heads together and find the hack who's creating our problems." With those words she left the office.

Nate sank down at his desk, a frown tugging his features. It wasn't just some hapless hack that had managed to breech the main computer and break into the Utopia program and personal files. It had been somebody with considerable computer savvy.

From his bottom desk drawer he withdrew two magazines. Both were computer tech periodicals and each had an article on Kathryn Sanderson, AKA Tiger Tech. Born and raised in the Silicon Valley, in the last five years Kathryn had made a name for herself in catching computer criminals. She'd not only worked for big business, but had also consulted with several police departments as well.

Accompanying one of the articles was a small photo. Although the picture was a little bit fuzzy, it depicted a young woman with a slender face, large eyes and short brown hair.

The picture didn't do her justice. The way he remembered, her face was slender, but always animated with abundance of confidence, laughter and life. There was no way a photo could capture the exact color of her hazel eyes, for they were always changing…sometimes blue…sometimes green, and always sparkling.

And that short brown hair was shot through with sun-kissed highlights that glistened and shone, adding a multitude of dimension to the color of brown.

He slammed the magazine shut and stuffed it back in hi
bottom drawer. He'd told her goodbye five years ago an
had assumed he'd never see her again. He didn't want t
see her again. She'd been the one risk he'd taken in hi
life…the one and only gamble he'd been willing to take
He didn't take risks anymore…the outcome was far to
painful.

He frowned and rolled his shoulders to release some o
the tension that had taken root in a spot in the center of hi
shoulder blades.

All he needed was a little more time and he could figure
out where the breech in the program was coming from a
on his own.

He punched up his computer, all set to get to work
Maybe he could have the problem solved before Tiger Tec
even got off her plane. Then she could just climb on th
next flight back to California.

He'd only been working for a minute or two when an
other knock on his door broke his concentration. "Com
in," he said in frustration.

Carmella Lopez, Executive Assistant to Lloyd Winters
entered carrying a fruit basket tied up in a pretty cello
phane. She smiled, her natural warmth radiating in th
depths of her chocolate brown eyes.

"Mr. Winters thought it would be nice if you'd give thi
to Ms. Sanderson when she arrives." She set the bountifu
basket on the coffee table in front of the sofa.

"How nice," Nate said, trying to ignore the irritatio
that rose inside him. Maybe he should just roll a red carpe
as well. Certainly everyone in the entire place seemed eage
to make Kat feel welcome. "I'm sure she'll appreciate it."

"We appreciate her coming all the way out here to hel
us," Carmella replied.

Nate knew he was being rather childish, but he couldn'
help it. Utopia was his baby and Lloyd and Emily Winter

were telling him to hand over his baby to the woman who'd once broken his heart. Of course, nobody knew about his former connection to Kat and he didn't intend to share the information with anyone.

Carmella glanced out the window where the snow was falling at a faster rate than last time he'd looked. "They've changed the forecast to four to eight inches by evening. I hope Ms. Sanderson knows how to dress for winter weather."

It was just like Carmella to worry about such a thing. She was always fretting over somebody. She often made Nate rather uncomfortable by straightening his tie or brushing lint off his jacket. He wasn't accustomed to being touched.

Carmella looked out the window once again and muttered something in Spanish beneath her breath. He gazed at her quizzically. She smiled. "I said, beautiful but treacherous. And now I'll let you get back to your work."

When she left Nate stared at the basket of fruit. The staff of Wintersoft Inc. could welcome Kathryn Sanderson to the fold all they wanted. But, they didn't have to work with her. He did.

Beautiful but treacherous, that not only described the snow falling outside the window, but could also apply to Kathryn Sanderson.

He walked over to the window and drew a deep breath, steeling himself for the experience of seeing her again.

SILHOUETTE *Romance*®

Three friends, three birthdays,
three loves of a lifetime!

if Wishes Were...

Discover what happens when wishes come true
in

BABY, OH BABY!

by Teresa Southwick
(Silhouette Romance #1704)

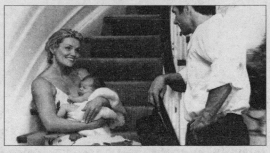

When Rachel Manning wished for a baby, she hadn't
expected to become an instant mother to an adorable
baby girl...or to share custody—and late-night feedings—
with the infant's maddeningly sexy, take-charge uncle!

Available January 2004 at your favorite retail outlet.

If you enjoyed what you just read,
then we've got an offer you can't resist!

Take 2 bestselling love stories FREE!
Plus get a FREE surprise gift!

Clip this page and mail it to Silhouette Reader Service

IN U.S.A.
3010 Walden Ave.
P.O. Box 1867
Buffalo, N.Y. 14240-1867

IN CANADA
P.O. Box 609
Fort Erie, Ontario
L2A 5X3

YES! Please send me 2 free Silhouette Romance® novels and my free surprise gift. After receiving them, if I don't wish to receive anymore, I can return the shipping statement marked cancel. If I don't cancel, I will receive 6 brand-new novels every month, before they're available in stores! In the U.S.A., bill me at the bargain price of $21.34 per shipment plus 25¢ shipping and handling per book and applicable sales tax, if any*. In Canada, bill me at the bargain price of $24.68 plus 25¢ shipping and handling per book and applicable taxes**. That's the complete price and a savings of at least 10% off the cover prices—what a great deal! I understand that accepting the 2 free books and gift places me under no obligation ever to buy any books. I can always return a shipment and cancel at any time. Even if I never buy another book from Silhouette, the 2 free books and gift are mine to keep forever.

209 SDN DU9H
309 SDN DU9J

Name	(PLEASE PRINT)	
Address	Apt.#	
City	State/Prov.	Zip/Postal Code

* Terms and prices subject to change without notice. Sales tax applicable in N.Y.
** Canadian residents will be charged applicable provincial taxes and GST.
   All orders subject to approval. Offer limited to one per household and not valid to current Silhouette Romance® subscribers.
   ® are registered trademarks of Harlequin Books S.A., used under license.

SROM03   ©1998 Harlequin Enterprises Limited

SILHOUETTE *Romance*®

COMING NEXT MONTH

#1702 RULES OF ENGAGEMENT—Carla Cassidy
Marrying the Boss's Daughter
Nate Leeman worked best alone, yet Wintersoft's senior VP now found himself the reluctant business partner to computer guru—and ex-girlfriend—Kat Sanderson. The hunky executive knew business and pleasure didn't mix. So why was he suddenly looking forward to long hours and late nights with his captivating co-worker?

#1703 THE BACHELOR BOSS—Julianna Morris
Sweet virgin Libby Dumont's former flame was now her boss? She'd shared one far-too-intimate kiss with the confirmed bachelor a decade ago, and although Neil O'Rourke was as handsome as ever, she knew he must remain off-limits. She just had to focus on business—*not* Neil's knee-weakening kisses!

#1704 BABY, OH BABY!—Teresa Southwick
If Wishes Were…
When Rachel Manning spoke her secret wish—to have a baby—she never expected to become an instant mother. She didn't even have a boyfriend! Yet here she was, temporary parent for a sweet month-old infant. Until Jake Fletcher—the baby's take-charge, heartbreaker-in-a-Stetson-and-jeans uncle—showed up and suggested sharing more than late-night feedings….

#1705 THE BABY CHRONICLES—Lissa Manley
Aiden Forbes was in trouble! He hadn't seen Colleen Stewart since she walked out on him eight years ago. Now he had been teamed with the marriage-shy journalist to photograph an article on babies, and seeing Colleen surrounded by all these adorable infants was giving Aiden ideas about a baby of their own!

SRCNM1203